TO JILT A CORINTHIAN

FRIENDSHIP SERIES BOOK 12

by Julia Donner

Cover Design by Stephen D Case and Tristan Case
Stephen@casegrfx.com

ISBN: 9781726658928

Please visit my website: www.MLRigdon.com
Blog: http://historyfanforever.wordpress.com/
Twitter: @RigdonML

The Friendship Series

The Tigresse and the Raven
The Heiress and the Spy
The Rake and the Bishop's Daughter
The Duchess and the Duelist
The Dark Earl and His Runaway
The Dandy and the Flirt
Lord Carnall and Miss Innocent
The Barbarian and His Lady
A Rogue for Miss Prim
An American for Agnes
A Laird's Promise
More Than a Milkmaid (2019)

"Julia Donner did it again! A smart, sassy heroine who's more interested in books than husband hunting, and a hero who does his best to stay one step ahead of her to win her heart. A delightful read!" *Judi Lynn, Mill Pond Romances*

Excerpt from *More Than a Milkmaid*, the next book in the series is included.

For Linda. It's not the same without you.

To Jilt a Corinthian   *Julia Donner*

Chapter 1

There was nothing else for it. Beatrice couldn't ignore Mrs. Pritchard's distress. The elderly widow sat on a wooden chair placed beside the doorstep of her wisteria-draped cottage. She wept loud and copious tears into the apron pressed over her face. All that could be seen of the dear lady's head was her bountiful, ruffled cap.

Having just come from the village, Beatrice switched the brown paper-wrapped parcel to her left hand in order to place a comforting palm on Mrs. Pritchard's shoulder. "Please, ma'am, how may I be of service to you?"

The widow uncovered her face and blinked swollen eyes to focus. "Oh, tis you, Miss Allardyce. How good of you to offer, but I am afraid my plight is not one for a lady to remedy." She pointed a gnarled forefinger at the enclosed area beyond the fence where a piglet squealed. "It's my little Scrumpy. The naughty boy escaped and found his way inside, just there, you see? Where he's gotten in?"

"Yes. There is quite a gap in the fencing. His pen is behind your cottage then?"

"Oh, no. He stays in a box in my kitchen. He's so very young, you see."

Beatrice peered over the fence and eyed the noisy piglet. "He appears to have caught his hind leg in

6

something. Twine or a thin rope perhaps. It's difficult to see. The area is quite overgrown."

"Oh, what shall I do, Miss Allardyce? My poor, poor Scrumpy. He was a gift from Farmer Winters."

"Calm yourself, Mrs. Pritchard. This is what we shall do. If you will please assist by holding my parcel?" Beatrice untied bonnet ribbons. "And my hat?" She peeled off the pale blue gloves that matched her bonnet and placed them on top of the package on Mrs. Pritchard's lap.

"But my dear, Miss Allardyce, what are you about? The gate is rusted shut and the fence impossible to climb."

"Not to worry, ma'am. Even so, I shall persevere."

Beatrice knelt in front of the gap in the fence amid further protests that she would ruin her muslin frock or cause a rip in the tight-fitting spencer, which happened to be Beatrice's favorite. Due to its snug fit, she was able to squeeze her body through the slats. She attempted to wriggle through until stopped by the curve of her hips. The indent of her waist allowed for room to breathe. Stretching as far as possible, held snug by the wooden slats, she managed to grab the piglet's front leg and drag him closer. Scrumpy squealed louder. Once the piglet was no longer forcing the tangled rope around his leg to be drawn tight and taut, Beatrice got the knotted twine unfastened and slipped it over the tiny, cloven foot. The pig immediately calmed to making soft grunts.

Beatrice exhaled a relieved sigh and carefully maneuvered a retreat from between the slats, but got stuck with the dilemma of how to maintain a hold on the piglet whilst wriggling back out. To her profound

7

dismay, she heard Mrs. Prichard call out to someone. Beatrice couldn't imagine anything more humiliating than getting caught on her hands and knees with her back end and nothing else exposed to the world.

She struggled gamely until Mrs. Pritchard said, "Oh, sir! Sir, would you kindly assist my dear Miss Allardyce? If you would take my piglet from her, I do believe she can bring herself through the fence."

A hand encased in a tan driving glove appeared from over the fence and reached by Beatrice's cheek to take the pig from her grasp. The next thought that entered her head was that the gentleman had to be tall to reach over the fence so easily. As she twisted sideways with breath indrawn, she heard Mrs. Pritchard expressing a joyous reunion with her pet.

Face burning, Beatrice extricated herself from between the fence and accepted the gloved palm waiting to assist her to her feet. She tried to keep her eyes cast downward but it was difficult not to notice what stood before her as she rose up. Dread filled her being. This was no villager.

She first noted the sparkle of black top boots that identified the particular care of a gentleman's gentleman. Then came the snug fit of immaculate breeches seen through the parting of an unfastened, ankle-length greatcoat. The drape of its superior cloth proclaimed it cost enough to feed a dozen families for a year. She looked higher. His preference of Brummel-austere style was made known with the subtle statement of only one fob draped across a black waistcoat secured by a golden pocket chain. His linen glowed bright in the sunlight. The three-caped greatcoat he wore had the graceful drape of the finest wool, its three layers

8

enhancing breadth of shoulders. When she stood fully upright, he removed a monocle, allowing it to hang from its black ribbon, and dipped his head in a nod of greeting.

Beatrice, achingly aware of the disheveled state of her person, dipped a curtsey. "My thanks for your assistance, sir."

"It was entirely my pleasure, Miss Allardyce."

If only a crevice in the earth would open up and swallow her whole, but before that wish could present itself, Mrs. Pritchard spoke up. "You are indeed an answer to prayer! Please forgive my curiosity, but I do not believe you are from Bruntwich-on-Lye."

"You are correct, ma'am. I am waiting for a small repair to my curricle before pressing on to London."

"I have never been, you know," Mrs. Pritchard coyly informed, cuddling her pet to her bosom. Scrumpy nestled against her, his little pink snout twitching with contentment. After being the cause of one of the most humiliating moments of her life, Beatrice was ready to toss the spoiled swine into the nearest cauldron.

A fresh wave of embarrassment swept through Beatrice when she noticed that her dirt-smeared hand had soiled the gentleman's tan glove. The front of her white muslin frock had mud smudges over the knees, its hem already grubby from taking a shorter route to the village through a sheep pasture. She felt entirely undone in the presence of this gentleman's perfection. She dared to glance up and encountered a cool gaze from hazel eyes under straight, black eyebrows. His was a lean and haughty face, making her glad he'd removed the monocle. Being viewed through that single lens would be worse than a minute inspection with a quizzing glass.

She'd always considered that practice a thoroughly rude affectation, but how could one complain about the use of a necessary aid—even if it did create more discomfort for the one being perused. This gentleman's sweeping and impersonal inspection made her nervous and his detached urbanity proved disconcerting. She offered a shallow curtsey in farewell and whirled to escape.

A silky baritone, lacquered with a vaguely mocking undertone, relayed volumes with two words. "Miss Allardyce?"

Forcing down a nervous swallow, she collected poise, turned, and lifted an eyebrow. He extended her package. She hadn't noticed it in his hand, distracted by embarrassment and feeling unsettled by the presence of so much masculine confidence and elegance. It was scarcely her fault that she'd never encountered a man so sophisticated. Her father's humble, priestly manner bore no resemblance to this sort of male.

She accepted the parcel, twitched a smile, and sought relief in the knowledge that it was unlikely she'd ever see him again, but he proved her wrong by attending Sunday service the following morning.

She sat in her usual spot, third pew from the front on the far left, chosen so that she could discreetly vacate the pew to join her father should he wish for her to stand with him at the doorway following the service. On occasion, she needed to return to the parsonage to set out luncheon, since Mrs. Holloway was often given Sundays off to spend with her husband.

Beatrice removed a small notebook from her

reticule. She usually daydreamed or construed poems during the sermon. She knew it by heart, having helped her father with its construction. Friday and Saturday were for perfecting the sermon. Her father's eyesight was starting to fail and she had the better penmanship and grammar skills. He was gifted with a perpetually kind and generous heart, but unfortunately, he lacked imagination when it came to writing anything that resembled a coherent homily. He provided her with verses and subject. She dashed off words for him to correct and provide his final decision.

While jotting down a few poem ideas during the prelude, she noticed the arrival of the Darcourts, whose family reserved the first pew on the right side of the aisle, the Viscount Brissard's across the aisle on the left.

Jonathan, Lord Darcourt, nodded a courteous bow in her direction as he passed, seating his wife and daughter in the family pew first. A visitor he'd brought with him sat on the aisle end of the pew. There was no mistaking their guest. The witness to yesterday's mortifying incident wore a black jacket so perfectly tailored that the material stretched across his upper back. Hatless, his seal dark hair was thick and obedient, not daring to show where the hat had rested. An odd urge to muss its perfection took her by surprise. Stranger still, her always active imagination pictured an unlikely image of him sitting casually, leaning back, shirt undone, a boot heel braced on the chair seat, an arm propped on his knee, his wealth of hair mussed under an amused, lazy-eyed stare.

The notebook she'd been holding slipped from her fingers, creating a sound that clacked throughout the

11

sanctuary. Rising up from collecting it from the floor, she encountered an aloof study of her disturbance, monocle in place, gaze impersonal but conveying reproach.

Heat crawled up her throat and into her cheeks. He must think her an idiot or a rustic willing to do anything for his august notice. When he returned his attention to her father stepping up to the pulpit, she feared that there was a hint of amusement lurking on the portion of his mouth that she could see. Drat the man. Even his profile had an arrogant, commanding aspect.

Putting him from her mind, she reopened the notebook and began to jot ideas. Immersed in her thoughts, the service went on without her. A loud chord announced the final hymn. She blinked, startled by how quickly time had passed, and stood. She sang without thinking, familiarity compensating for her flustered state.

A vibrant basso came from across the aisle. Mr. Monocle also sang without benefit of hymnal. His was the deep, resonating voice that mesmerized, the sort that sent tingles everywhere and made her imagine heated whispers of an indelicate nature.

She broke off singing, impatient with the theme of her ridiculous imagination. Of all things to be thinking about in church! She hurried out of the pew on the last verse to join her father. After he'd given the benediction at the back of the sanctuary, she fidgeted in place, trying to think of a reason to escape. The one she had in mind was to beg leave to prepare luncheon, but he stayed her with a smile and by taking her hand.

He spoke in an undertone before the parishioners reached them. "Squire Cartwright's invitation. Have you forgotten? And I believe Lord Darcourt has a guest he would wish to introduce. Don't fidget, my dear."

It was impossible to deny her father's dulcet request. His persistent kindly tone and gentle character precluded argument. Obedience came naturally and had been so all of her life. She'd never been able to deny him anything. The thought of disappointing him in any way brought to the surface tears and crushing regret. It was little different for her father. His affable personality and tender heart collapsed in the presence of any display of cruelty or base behavior. But where he had been blessed with bottomless patience and kindness, she struggled with a belligerent streak that required constant vigilance to counteract unseemly outbursts and behaviors, such as the one she now nursed—a naughty urge to render the Darcourt's aloof visitor appalled and undone with a cunning remark. Nothing cutting, mind you, something clever and…sophisticated. Something brilliant to prove she's wasn't a rustic mouse.

As parishioners filed by, shaking hands and exchanging pleasantries, she nursed another worry that pushed aside the awkwardness of what had occurred the day before with Mrs. Pritchard's pig extraction. What if Darcourt's guest dealt her sweet-natured father a dose of his snobbery? Corinthians came in all sizes and attitudes. This one's sangfroid was as impenetrable as a block of ice. Why then had she pictured him earlier in such a state of undress, lounging and relaxed, the exact opposite of—

"Good morning, Miss Beatrice!"

Hearing her name, she jerked back to the present. Lord Darcourt smiled pleasantly, so did his wife, by his

13

side, clutching his arm.

Beatrice found her wits and her voice. "And to you, Jonathan. How are you, Emily?"

Her friend since childhood, Lady Darcourt gurgled a laugh. "Oh, Beatrice, we are so delighted to have a guest with us! Jonathan, do make the introductions."

Since they were standing just beyond the entrance, Lord Darcourt replaced his hat and placed his freed hand over his wife's grip on his arm. "Calm, my dear. And so I shall. Reverend, I should like to present to you a fellow classmate from university days. This is Sir Joceyln Warfield. Joss, this is our most admirable vicar, Reverend Howard Allardyce and his daughter, Miss Beatrice Allardyce."

Far from presenting a frosty front, Sir Joceyln nodded before reseating the hat he held and extending his hand. "How very good to meet you, sir. Your sermon held my attention throughout. Such distinctive alliteration and flowing style are not usually found at the pulpit."

Her doting father, on the verge of giving her the credit, halted when she nudged his side with her elbow. The Darcourts missed the move, but unfortunately, Sir Jocelyn didn't. The golden in his hazel eyes gleamed in the sunlight. Yesterday, she'd thought they were brownish, not this arresting combination of colors. His gaze still contained a coldness she could not like.

Her heart thumped when he directed that impersonal yet penetrating stare at her. "How is the pig?"

Startled, she blurted, "Where are your manners?"

Her father inhaled and made a distressing noise as Sir Jocelyn half-smiled and replied, "Left them behind
14

when I came upon a troublemaker sneaking through a fence."

She fired back, "It was an act of mercy, sir, as I am sure you are well aware."

This time, there was no mistaking his smile when he suavely replied, "It was an act of mercy that I shall never forget, Miss Allardyce. Did you sustain an injury?"

Caught off guard again, she blinked. "Uhm, no. How kind of you to ask. I think."

"Shouldn't wish to deal a slight to a pig's rescuer."

Miffed that he'd somehow gotten the upper hand, she muttered, "Indeed, one would not."

Her tone had gone from cool to acerbic, causing another flicker of interest in his, amusement or scorn, she couldn't tell. What clearly registered was that she would love to pierce that brittle shell. For a delicious moment, she imagined dealing his booted shin a decisive kick just for the satisfaction of watching him wince—then was appalled by the violence of her emotions. What was wrong with her? The man was annoyingly arrogant, but so were most of his kind.

Even though engaged in a glaring contest with Sir Jocelyn, she'd been acutely aware of three pairs of eyes shifting back and forth between their shuttling comments, as if watching a tennis match.

When she opened her mouth to turn the conversation, Jonathan Darcourt, ever the pacifier, quickly inserted, "Reverend, Miss Beatrice, will you join us for a late luncheon?"

Her father answered, "How very kind, but I regret that we have accepted a previous invitation. Will you be staying in the neighborhood long, Sir Jocelyn?"

"I had planned to stay only for the time it took to repair an axle, then I had the great good fortune to encounter Jonathan at the blacksmith's. He and his wife extended an invitation to visit."

Beatrice kept her mouth firmly shut as her father said, "I do hope you will visit with us longer. I should like to further our acquaintance."

"As would I," Sir Jocelyn replied, but he was looking at her.

Chapter 2

To save time, they took the path through the cemetery to the parsonage to collect the pony cart. "Father, I wish you would not encourage that man."

Holding up his gown and surplice hem, he said, "Do you speak of Sir Jocelyn, my dear?"

"But of course, Father. He's frightfully…oh, I don't know. Perhaps too full of himself, or what is the saying…sangfroid. And too full of his own consequence."

"Hush, now, child. We must consider that he must reflect his upbringing. These great men are often left at the mercy of their environments."

"Forgive me, Father, but do I hear you making excuses for his snobbery? He's not a royal duke or the like."

"No, but he is a personage of some note. I have read of him in the newspapers. He has been given much praise for his speeches in Parliament."

"Undoubtedly a Tory," she muttered ungraciously.

"A Whig, actually. Since assuming his brother's title, he's aligned himself with the Asterly conclave."

Disgruntled that her father wouldn't join in with her rant about associating with Sir Jocelyn, she resorted to silence as they walked up the pathway to the parsonage door, where her father paused and turned to look out over the countryside lush with the green of early summer.

Warning bells clanged inside her head when her

father announced, quite pleased with himself, "I shall invite them to dinner."

Numbed by this, she almost tumbled off the doorstep. "Papa, the expense! You must know that they are the sort who expect a lavish table."

He lifted her limp hand for an avuncular pat. "Not to worry, my girl. Squire Bellows promised to send over a brace of grouse, and Mrs. Holloway mentioned a joint of lamb was to be delivered this week. We must give thanks for yet another generous gift from a congregation member. There should be enough for a pottage. How I do so love lamb stew. Remind me to get the parishioner's name and we shall send a note. The asparagus is doing quite well and there are some early root vegetables. There you have your menu, dear child. Simple as that."

"But Papa—"

As he ushered her inside, he added, "And your mother's best dinner service can be brought down, and you shall prepare the trifle the way she showed you. I defy anyone to prepare a trifle with your gift."

And that was how she came to be in the kitchen prior to the arrival of the Darcourts, Sir Jocelyn and another couple visiting with them. Her father invited Widow Beardsley to even the numbers. The small dining room looked acceptable but on the edge of a squeeze with the need to seat eight. The flowers freshly picked graced the table and candles stood ready for lighting, which were the frightfully dear beeswax and mustn't be lit until the last moment.

Mrs. Holloway had everything in order and her son, Henry, who had experience working in the larger homes in the district, had agreed to serve. The kitchen smelled divine with the aromas of all that baked, roasted, and simmered, making her empty stomach grumble in anticipation. At her shoulder, Mrs. Holloway whipped cream and hummed a happy tune.

Beatrice tied a voluminous apron over her dress and checked the ingredients set out on the kitchen's wood block. Sponge cake and plump raspberries waited for assembly. A bottle of her father's favorite madeira stood open and breathing beside the last bottle of their best sherry. She tasted the port and found it mellow and ready. Next came the layering of the sponge and drizzling port over the cake. While that rested for a moment, she tasted the sherry. Her father loved port but her preference was sherry, and she would be sad to see the end of this bottle. The tumbler she'd used for sampling the madiera stood empty. She poured in a dollop of sherry, judged its excellent color and sipped while finishing up the trifle's assembly. Before dropping the last of the berries on top of the final layer of whipped cream, she noticed the tumbler of sherry empty and splashed in a last taste.

Mrs. Holloway came to judge the final product. "My word, Miss Beatrice, that looks fine."

"Yesh...I mean, quite. How goes the meal?"

Mrs. Holloway wiped her hands on her apron and propped them on her broad hips. "All is ready, miss. Henry has the wines opened and lined up in order. The grouse are browning nicely and the lamb joint should be ready by the time the guests are seated."

"Share a glass with me. This sherry is...marshal...marvelous."

Henry poked his head into the kitchen. "Miss Beatrice, your father said to fetch you. The Darcourt carriage has arrived."

The passageway to the front of the parsonage looked a bit fuzzy but amusingly so, bringing about a contented smile and happy hum that buzzed inside her head as she made her way to the parsonage's modest foyer. How fortunate that she'd had a bit of sherry to calm her nerves. The pleased smile stayed in place as she welcomed guests with her father. She scarcely noticed Sir Jocelyn, who'd been seated to her left and Lord Darcourt, dear Jonathan, on her right. Dear Emily sat by her father and the widow.

She had a vague impression of time passing. Eating food that had lost its taste. From her vantage point at one end of the table, everyone appeared to be having a quite pleasant evening. Compliments for the cook came with each course. Her father's selection of wines were discussed and appreciated.

An unfamiliar couple were in attendance. She didn't recall seating them center table and now struggled to think through the fuzziness to recall their names. Surely they'd been introduced.

"You're squinting," a deep voice murmured. It couldn't be Jonathan. He was always jovial and his voice pitched higher.

Blinking, she confronted the comment, "Bed…I mean, beg your pardon?"

"Miss Allardyce, you are positively glaring at Lady Richardson."

She felt a frown wrinkling her forehead. She redirected her annoyance at the man wearing a monocle, seated on her left. Father must have put him there, when she'd wanted him center table. "So thash her nem."

20

That was an unfortunate slip, allowing her words to go mushy like that. And more than a little annoying. When she reached for the wine glass, a foot lightly kicked the side of her slipper. Since it came from the left, the culprit had to be Sir Jocelyn. That wouldn't do.

It was imperative to carefully focus on every word. "No apology, sir?"

She'd thought that his peering at her with that intimidating and judgmental monocle was the worst anyone could suffer, but as it turned out, it wasn't. His cold, sure smile was more daunting. And irritating.

The thought came and went of tossing the remainder of the wine in his face. No, Father wouldn't like that at all. And she supposed it might make an awkward moment for his guests. Father looked so very pleased at the other end of the table, beaming at the company, chatting, and enjoying himself. There was nothing else for it. She looked Sir Jocelyn right in the monocle'd eye. Hidden by the safety of the table linens, she dealt him a hard kick on the shin.

Chapter 3

The direct hit to his shinbone was no ladylike blow. Pain streaked up to his knee. Joss smiled at his hostess as she smiled, all innocence, and took a dainty sip of wine. Already deep in her cups, he was looking forward with more than a little relish to see if she found herself able to stand and walk in a straight line, or even remain upright when it was time for the ladies to leave the room.

He never would have imagined that any form of enjoyment could be had at dinner in a rustic village. The idea boggled credulity, and yet, here he was at table in a rural shire. Lady Richardson, a high stickler of the first order and inordinately proud of the fact that she was invited to all of the best houses in London, had not been able to conceal her horror of the situation. Her expression fairly shouted that she and her bored husband had been transported to social hell by the well-meaning Darcourts. Tender-hearted Lady Darcourt was presently doing her best to conceal her concern for Miss Allardyce.

Last evening, Jonathan's wife had gone on at length about her dearest and very talented friend, Miss

Allardyce, and yet their hostess and her supposedly clever friend had said next to nothing throughout the duration of the meal. What she did manage was a mumbled sentence about cooking pork. The rest of her conversation sounded simple-minded when not monosyllabic.

He should be grateful that he was no longer hungry. The fare was plain, uninspired to say the least, but on the other hand, the grouse and lamb, although plainly dressed, were quite beautifully rendered. And he particularly liked fowl and lamb.

Poor Lady Darcourt had been diligently striving to garner her friend's attention, although how that could be achieved Joss would never imagine. Miss Allardyce's dreamy expression and occasionally crossed eyes made it apparent that she was decidedly inebriated. It wouldn't be the first time he'd attended an event with a drunken hostess, but the condition usually occurred toward the end of the meal, after the various wines that accompanied many courses. There had been only two wines so far this evening, one served with the grouse and the other with the lamb. He supposed another would come at the last, and supposed correctly, when a trifle was presented.

Reverend Allardyce announced, "This is my late wife's receipt, who taught my daughter its secret ingredients."

Everyone politely raised their glasses to the

hostess, who continued to smile in dazed, drunken content. After a taste of the confection, he discovered what the secret involved—a great deal of spirits. The lot of them might end up knocked off their pins with one serving.

After the sweet and wine were consumed, everyone looked to the hostess. Joss gave her slipper another nudge and she scowled in his direction. Fortunately, reality and responsibility permeated her befuddled state. She blinked and smiled at the footman. "Henry, coffee in the drawing room, please."

Joss steeled himself to stay his hand from assisting his hostess as Miss Allardyce stood. She corrected her list to the right by bracing her palms flat on the table. Amazingly, she stayed upright as the women left the room. Her loyal friend, Lady Darcourt, insinuated a steadying hand under her elbow.

The gentlemen retook their seats. He declined to smoke but did take port. He presumed that he'd already sampled it, thinking it might be that same tolerable sort used in the trifle. And it was, he was happy to discover. He liberally indulged, since he owned a much harder head than poor Miss Allardyce. He missed her company, perhaps due to the amusement she provided during dinner.

The memory of her bottom wriggling between the fence slats made him smile, which he hastily erased. The political discussion in progress didn't denote anything humorous. Soon, they would ask his opinion. How tiresome.

It was an ever boggling notion that anyone should be interested in what he thought regarding a particular issue, especially when taking into account that he had no interest in anyone else's opinion. Mayhap his interest was due to the fact that their opinions came into being by listening to the thoughts of others. With the exception of the priest, none in the room had a viable idea between the lot of them. He was quite fond of Darcourt, but his friend had been a dull student in school and proved himself shockingly ill-informed every time he stood up in Parliament. Nevertheless, Jonathan's jovial nature and sweetness of character rendered him necessary to counteract his own pessimistic bent.

The reverend brought up his daughter's name, drawing Joss from his lackluster attention to the conversation. The man had acted totally unaware of his daughter's drunken state and made it abundantly clear that in his opinion she was perfection. Indeed, Lady Darcourt had attested to many unsubstantiated comments about Miss Allardyce. Nothing the young lady had done this evening proved her to be the epitome of all that was wonderful when it came to womanhood. She did possess a fine pair of eyes—that unusual shade of pale blue that readily changed depending on the color worn. This evening, her frock's cerulean silk brightened the blue. The other day, her hair had been covered by a bonnet and under its brim, the ruffled frill of a cap. Dark blond eyebrows didn't reveal much, but tonight, under the candlelight, flaxen streaks gleamed amid the tawny brown. He imagined she would look entirely blond in the sunlight.

Chair legs scraped, prompting him to stand with the men on the way to join the ladies. He wouldn't be surprised to catch his hostess snoring on a corner sofa. That would supply some diversion. If Miss Alardyce would not be so obliging, he might take the reverend aside for some intelligent conversation. The man's sermon last Sunday had moments of brilliance.

Alas, Miss Allardyce was not obliging. She did look a bit ashen about the gills but gamely saw to the arranging of tables for cards. Jonathan, his wife, Lady Richardson, whose husband was actually snoring on the corner sofa, and the pleasant Mrs. Beardsley had already made up a set and were about to deal out the cards. The reverend sat next to the widow, in order to give her direction.

Joss was about to stroll over to the card table when he saw Miss Allardyce make a beeline exit. He followed her out, maintaining his casual gait until achieving the passage, where he caught a glimmer of blue at its end. He picked up his pace and looked into the room where she'd fled just in time to see her fly through a glass-paned garden door. Striding across what appeared to be a morning room, he arrived outside to see her stumble. She caught the rim of a low wall and might have pitched forward over it had he not reached out to stop the fall. Instead of his hand finding her waist, a breast filled his palm as she cast up the little dinner she'd eaten and a great deal of wine.

Chapter 4

A calm, deep voice filtered through her bleary vision. She couldn't rightly distinguish the words, could only register the relief of getting rid of the swirling contents of her stomach. A cloth dabbed at her mouth. The words became understandable.

"Miss Allardyce, are you able to stand on your own?"

She blinked away blurriness, and after a moment, realized that she was out-of-doors and it was night. The prop of something warm and solid provided a welcome foundation for the shivering that had overtaken her limbs. A man held her. He felt sturdy, nothing like her father's bony frame.

"Please, Miss Allardyce, can you stand on your own? There is someone observing us from the window."

Clarity returned in a rush when he slipped his hand from around her waist. Murky yellow light poured from the nearby window and glowed on rhododendron leaves. She wrapped trembling fingers around the forearm he offered and stepped away from his side.

"Thank you, sir. I am much improved."

"I would agree, if not for the fact that all color is

leached from your face. Perhaps I could fetch something to drink."

She huffed a derisive laugh. "I believe I've had enough for one evening."

"For an entire week, I should think," he murmured.

She wobbled a bit when she let go of his arm. "My head may be whirling but there is nothing amiss with my hearing."

"Beg pardon."

"That doesn't sound even remotely remorseful."

"I admit to an inability to varnish the truth," he added, cupping a hand under her elbow, and such was her weakened state that she allowed it.

"One can refrain from comment, sir, and I will have you know that it has not been my life ambition to humiliate myself in front of guests. One can only pray that Father didn't see this."

"He didn't, but Lady Richardson most certainly did."

She pressed a palm to her brow. "Oh, devil take it."

"What did you just say?"

She inhaled a fortifying breath and leaned away from him, impatient that she could never keep a leash on the connection from brain to mouth. When she groped for the edge of the terrace wall, he intercepted her hand.

"Not there, Miss Allardyce."

Resigned but not cowed, she turned away from the unpleasantness of where she would have placed her hand and looked up. "Do I hear censure in your tone?"

"Never censure, ma'am, surely not, but merely a hint of warning. Especially in regard to Lady Richardson."

"Whatever could the woman or anyone else find wrong with a Samaritan act?"

"It is not the kindness itself but perhaps the accidental placement of my assistance."

Now restored to her proper self, she glanced over her shoulder at the withdrawing room window that provided a view of the narrow terrace and garden. "You are mistaken, sir. There is no one at the window."

"Not now. As I said, she left. Smirking."

"What sort of person finds amusement in another's misery."

"I doubt she was amused. More likely elated to have discovered a gaffe."

Unhappy that it was necessary to continue to avail herself of his supporting arm, she carefully moved toward the door left ajar. "I can see no reason for elation."

"Then you are not familiar with her sort. Lady Richardson is a known gossip. I believe she may have seen where I inadvertently placed my hand."

"I've no idea what you are talking about, and why should the universe come to a shrieking halt merely because you had your hand on my waist?"

He closed the door she'd gone through and faced her. The monocle now hung from its ribbon. "You were distressed, your focus elsewhere, leaving you unaware of where my hand accidentally landed, but one must also take into consideration that we are unaccompanied."

Faculties restored, she lifted her eyebrows. "Sir, you do not suggest that I created a situation of compromise."

"Miss Allardyce, if any other female were involved, the idea might enter my mind. But in your case, no."

"Then we will hear no more of it, sir. But I do thank you for your assistance."

Guests were waiting and no doubt wondering what had happened. She brushed aside their concerns by confessing to feeling momentarily unwell and requiring a breath of air. Kindness was expressed all around, but Lady Richardson's smug grin hinted at something unpleasant. The woman might make mischief. Well, let her. No one in the parish would believe the tittle-tattle of an outsider.

The following morning she awoke with no painful aftereffects and had slept soundly but late. Her father was finishing luncheon and the newspaper when she joined him. Tea was all she could manage. Her stomach had settled but her appetite had not returned.

Pouring tea, she asked, "Have you given thought to Sunday's homily?"

He lowered the paper and smiled tiredly. "I will think on it later today. I must visit the McIntires. They've not yet come through the loss of her brother."

Her hand remained on the teapot handle as she absorbed the man sitting beside her. Weariness mantled his person, weighing down his usually erect posture. His eyes, the same color as hers, had paled to a watery blue-green, fading with the film of aging. He looked thinner, more fragile, and somehow defeated.

When he folded and set the newspaper aside, she wrapped her fingers around his bony wrist. "Papa, was last evening too much for you?"

"No, daughter, but it did bring into perspective something I have been ignoring. Rather selfishly, I should think."

"Nonsense, Papa. There is no person in this world as kind and thoughtful as you."

His half smile held the hint of failure. Worry twisted her heart when his gaze met hers. Intuition warned her that his mood had less to do with age and weariness than the weight of a serious issue. Premonition whispered that whatever plagued her father, whatever he was about to say, would change the course of their world.

His cool, dry palm covered hers. "Beatrice, I had a visitor this morning. The caller came quite unexpectedly and early."

"Oh, no. A parishioner in difficulty?"

"Not a parishioner." His hesitation launched heartbeats that throbbed inside her head then ceased when he said, "Sir Jocelyn came to ask permission for your hand in marriage."

That revelation emptied her mind and stopped time. She stared, feeling as if she'd been flung into an imaginary realm, a dimension where nothing made sense. Indeed, there were times when she became so engrossed in whatever she was writing that she felt outside of herself, but this was quite different. She realized that later on understanding would set in and logic would prevail, but at this moment, her father's words were incomprehensible.

"Beatrice, have I shocked you out of countenance? This is not the first time you have been asked for, although by no one as illustrious as the baronet."

Yet numb, she mumbled, "There was Jonathan."

"We knew that he wasn't serious. Merely a lark to make Emily sit up and take notice, don't you think? The other four were nice enough young men. Of course, the Holland boy and Mrs. Prichards's nephew would not do for someone with your education, and you insisted in every instance that no one could replace your papa."

"And Henry Sheffield didn't approve of my learning Latin and Greek." A sudden thought collected her scattered wits. She sent her father a beseeching look. "You can't think that I would ever abandon you, Father."

His hand squeezed hers before withdrawing it. "I have overset you by telling you this without preamble and am sorry for that, but there seemed no other way than to just tell you. It did astonish me, having him ask for you after such short acquaintance. It has given me food for thought...about the future."

"Papa, you need never worry that I would leave you. In any event, I scarcely know the man and have never entertained ideas of marriage. You must have told him that I have little in the way of dowry."

"That didn't alter his insistence that his request was honorably and sincerely presented, and my dear, the summary of his holdings that came with the baronetcy was most impressive as are his future expectations. And one cannot dismiss his intelligence. We exchanged an excellent conversation. I believe he would seek out your opinion and showed remarkable acceptance of your unusual education."

"Conversation would be a prerequisite for me but that is scarcely enough to entice me to accept a marriage proposal."

"He presented a convincing display of a man who has made an irrevocable decision. Did he anticipate this morning's interview by pressing his suit with you?"

She thought back to the previous evening. "Not

really. There was some foolishness about being alone on the terrace, but I assured him that it was of no consequence."

"And you were unwell. That is why I am entirely put out with myself this morning. My dear Bea, you will forgive this neglectful parent for not noticing that you were ill, won't you?"

"It was nothing, Father, exactly as I told everyone."

"But I was so involved with Mrs. Beardsley that I neglected to give you the attention you required. Too wrapped in my own concerns and happiness. I should never have been so neglectful. Shamefully so."

"Papa, stop this! It was nothing. A simple muddle, and what do you hint at regarding the widow?"

"We shall speak of that later. How shall I respond to Sir Jocelyn's request? Keep in mind that this year you turn twenty-seven."

She dropped sugar lumps in the tea and briskly stirred. After a taste of too sweet tea, logic and equilibrium returned. She added more tea to dilute the sweetness.

"You must not bother yourself with this, Papa. I shall drive the pony cart over to Lowbridge Hall on the pretense of visiting Emily. While there, I shall take Sir Jocelyn aside and ask him to desist."

Her father sent her a leery glance and looked down to fiddle with a spoon that he began to turn around and around. "Daughter, I fear that Sir Jocelyn is a man not easily swayed. There is a particular steadiness about him. He went so far as to ask to have the banns read on Sunday."

That made her stop stirring. She set down the spoon and took a sip while organizing a strategy. Sir Jocelyn wasn't in the room but nonetheless still managed to make mischief. The man was too overwhelming, a too large presence in their lives.

"That sort of presumption will not do, Father. You shall leave it to me, and when I return, we will have a lovely chat about the sermon and put all of this behind us."

How easily that rolled off her tongue, but on the drive to enlist Emily's aid, she had no idea how to confront this problem. Sir Jocelyn was nothing like the other suitors who attempted to take her away from her father and suggest that she abandon writing and her studies, but as her father pointed out, he was intelligent. Sporting pursuits aside, he'd attended university with Jonathan and had made an impression with erudite speeches in Parliament. Surely he would respond to logic.

Chapter 5

She hadn't gotten through the front door at Lowbridge Hall long enough to remove her gloves when Emily came flying out of the drawing room.

"Oh, Bea, I knew you would come!"

Stalled while reaching to unfasten pelisse buttons, Beatrice was almost knocked off her feet by her friend's embrace. "Emily, what has you so overset?"

"And happy, too! Jonathan and I can't be more delighted. In transports, I tell you, but we are so worried about you."

"Why? I am in perfect health and temperament."

Emily gaped, confused, then blinked. "But are you not in the clouds? Joss is precisely the sort of husband for you."

"Whatever gave you that impression? I grant you, he is not stupid, but I've never been in favor of Corinthian pursuits."

"But all gentlemen participate in such activities, just as we adore shopping and visiting with one's friends. And Joss is so commanding. I wish you could have been here when he sent off Lady Richardson with a flea in her ear."

When Beatrice lifted her eyebrows with a question, Emily gleefully explained, "All the way home in the carriage she made the most disparaging remarks. Jonathan and I firmly disagreed, but she would not be dissuaded. Joss drove his curricle and didn't hear the worst of it. She foolishly continued when we got here. Oh, Bea, I feared Joss would lose his temper, but he only became colder and cut her down in the sharpest manner, but quietly, you know. The ice that slices to the bone. He warned her to say nothing more in regards to his intended, his *intended*. Oh, you could've knocked us over with a feather! You are engaged, my wonderful Bea. And you shall never need to worry about gossip when you take your place with him in London. Joss warned the harpy that he would know its source. What a horrid, horrid woman. Oh, Bea, please forgive us. Jonathan and I are so terribly sorry that we brought them to your dinner party. Relatives or not, Jonathan has sworn that they shall never cross our threshold again. Thank goodness they left at sunlight and we didn't have to suffer an awkward scene."

Beatrice had stood quietly absorbing her friend's outpouring. Emily wasn't the brightest apple in the bowl, but she was undoubtedly the sweetest. She regretted that she couldn't have dealt the wretched Lady Richardson and her equally dull husband with a tongue-lashing of her own. It was distressing that her closest friends had been made to feel guilty by the perpetrator of the worst sort of behavior. And while houseguests.

Beatrice gave her friend a cuddly hug and smiled her fondness as she withdrew. "It is a blessing beyond measure to have a loyal friend like you. I am terribly sorry that you were subjected to so much bother on my account."

"I vow they shall never cross our doorstep again."

Beatrice pinched her lips to hide a smile. Emily in a fit of righteous outrage looked more like a scowling kitten than the snarling tiger she wished to impart. "Please accept my gratitude and condolences. The adage of being at the mercy of those we must tolerate as relatives has never been truer. The Richardsons of this world can never aspire to your level of goodness. I thank you for your defense but must confess that I am neither moved nor impressed by the meanness of her tittle-tattle. Or anyone else's. Now, I have come to speak briefly with Sir Jocelyn."

"He and Jonathan went riding. Will you wait for him? I've so much to ask about your splendid news."

"Forgive me, Emily, but if he is out, I should like to invite myself back for tea later today, or if that is not convenient, tomorrow?"

Emily followed as Beatrice gestured for Price, the butler who hovered, to reopen the door. "But there is so much to talk about. Why not wait until they return?"

"I would, if not for an appointment with Father, and knowing men who love their horses, they may not come back until nightfall."

Emily followed when Beatrice went down the steps, pulling on her gloves as she descended. "Price," she called over her shoulder, "don't bother sending for my cart. It's probably not reached the stable yet."

Emily scampered ahead to block her way and captured Beatrice's hands. "Please, don't leave, Bea. And don't be angry with us."

"Don't be a pigeon-head, Emily." She pressed her cheek to Emily's. "There's nothing that you or Jonathan could *ever* possibly do to warrant anger on my part. Or anyone else's for that matter. There is no couple more thoughtful."

When Emily's pretty features creased with sudden apprehension and she shifted her gaze sideways, Beatrice shook her head. "How can you think otherwise? You are both too kind and generous. Now, allow me to be on my way. If you would be so good as to ask Sir Jocelyn to call on us."

Emily wailed under her breath. "Oh, you do plan to break it off!"

"I admit that he's been chivalrous, but that is not enough of a recommendation for me."

"Then you are disappointed that you haven't found love."

"Nonsense. Love is rarely a prerequisite for marriage. Only you and Jonathan are the exception."

The thuds of approaching horses halted her first step toward the stables. Two riders came up the incline out of the park at a canter. One burst forward into a gallop, heading directly at the stone wall that separated the topiary from the swath of lawn in front of the house. Turf clods flew as the muscular, chestnut hunter Sir Jocelyn rode charged the barrier. Jonathan had veered off to canter through the open gate farther down the lane, the

40

wiser option.

Man and beast lunged at the wall, the horse going airborne with a heaving grunt, its rider focused on her, not his mount. Beatrice had been about to retreat up the steps until she recognized Sir Joceyln. She stood her ground as Emily let out a muffled squeak and huddled against her back. The horse landed with a thump that resounded up through the soles of her shoes and came to a sliding halt near enough that the horse's scent and breath brushed over her face.

Sir Jocelyn kicked free of the irons and leaped down. A groom came running to take the reins he held out. A few strides brought him to them where he touched his hat brim.

"Good morrow to you, Miss Allardyce. Forgive the rushed arrival but I didn't wish to have you leave without speaking with you first. My apologies, Emily. Did I give you a fright?"

Hands still clutching Beatrice's shoulders, she peeked around to say, "Oh, Joss, I wouldn't have survived the fright had it not been for Beatrice. She was my shield. So like her, you know."

Beatrice stepped back to wrap a comforting arm around Emily's waist. "What happened to your monocle, sir? Lose it on that last jump?"

His reaction to her mild taunt was a narrowing of his eyes and a disconcerting gleam. "Never wear it while riding. Will you walk with me, Miss Allardyce, or would you prefer to go inside?"

Sensing that Emily hovered, eager for encouraging information, Beatrice answered, "A walk, sir. The day is fine, and it has come to my

41

understanding that we have matters to discuss."

Jonathan arrived and dismounted. "Blast it, Joss. No one has broached that fence since Father."

Emily waited until Jonathan's horse had been taken away to go to her husband and twine an arm though his. "Thank you for not attempting it."

Sir Jocelyn said to Jonathan, "You could have done on that chestnut gelding. He'd have easily cleared higher. You were right about him. I should like to buy him from you."

"Excellent," Emily said with her kittenish scowl. "Then he won't be tempted to try it!"

Sir Jocelyn answered that with a smile and the gentle tone he used only with Emily, "Then as your obedient servant, ma'am, the horse shall be mine and taken far from here. If you would excuse us, I believe Miss Allardyce and I have, as she said, matters to discuss."

Beatrice suffered an internal squirm when Emily and Jonathan shared a conspiratorial grin. She couldn't get away from the front of the house quick enough and gestured at the entrance to the topiary.

Neither of them spoke for a time. Sir Jocelyn watched the passage of the lawn beneath his boots, while she pretended to look at animal and geometrically shaped bushes.

When she paused to study what appeared to be a bear, he spoke first. "I presume you spoke with your father."

Here was another side of Sir Jocelyn Warfield. Her first impression had been to perceive him as haughty, a disinterested-in-others sort of person.

42

Then he'd been the soul of pragmatic patience during her embarrassing weakness on the terrace, neither squeamish nor scornful. Minutes before, he'd been considerate of Emily's tender sensibilities, and now—how could one best describe his present attitude? The comment about her father was actually a question offered up in a bland, contemplative monotone, a non-threatening fishing expedition.

She gave him an answer point blank, a fait accompli. "I thank you but your offer is entirely unwarranted."

"You may hold that opinion, and as much as I respect it, I would wish that you not...with so little forethought...cast aside my offer. I am familiar with the sort of mischief and damage a dedicated gossiper can achieve with the merest suggestion. Lady Richardson has a reputation as a scandalmonger and wields her tongue like a surgeon's knife. I will not be an accomplice when an innocent is ruined. One can be assured that whatever her poisonous language contrives, it will be all over town in a week."

"Sir, I will likely never set foot in London. Therefore, as much as I value your gentlemanly sentiments, I have no worries about my honor being besmirched."

"Then what about my own?"

She halted to look up at him and choked on the urge to laugh. "Sir, what man does not enjoy *that* sort of reputation?"

"Certainly not one like your father," came his quick, sardonic reply. "And please consider that

43

there is one's social standing, as opposed to reputations of an entirely different sort. There are clear distinctions, are there not? A man known for amatory pursuits with women of loose character, or with those no longer in…the first bloom, shall we say? I've taken into consideration that you are respectable, even revered in this community, and unmarried. That is an entirely different matter. We were seen alone, Miss Allardyce, in close physical contact, in a dark garden. Even with a chaperone, not easily disregarded."

He was right. She made an impatient noise and started walking again. "It is not a remedy that is fair to you, sir, and marriage does not correspond with my plans."

Strolling along by her side with his hands clasped behind his back, he again watched where his boots passed over the grass. "Might those plans involve taking care of your father, seeing to parish needs, and other interests?"

"By interests one must assume you mean my bluestocking problem."

He hummed a reply, and she snapped off a branch to whack at topiary art. "Since we speak of unfairness, Father is an excellent teacher and has blessed me with a passion for learning. I confess to unfeminine pastimes. I like to read and write in the privacy of my room. There is no harm in that, but one would think I am devising traitorous pamphlets for the masses."

"You write his sermons, don't you?"

"My preference is essays. One must have some form of outlet, and Father lost his calling for
44

dredging up homilies along with his eyesight."

"Perhaps that is why he didn't notice that you were drunk to the point of sliding off your chair."

She resisted the impulse to whack him with the branch. "Oh, I thank you kindly for resurrecting that charming scene. You must know that I had no idea how much I'd taken. I'm not a tippler and have never been inebriated in my life."

"I was well aware of that."

She halted abruptly to glare up at him. "I've asked you before, but must have it confirmed now, that you don't think that I planned to ensnare you in a compromising situation."

He looked directly at her. "Absolutely not."

His focused, hazel-eyed stare set off an internal alarm, one she'd never experienced before. She'd considered him cold and aloof, but that wasn't what she was seeing now. The barrier to his inner self was still in place, but the suggestion of strong emotions held fiercely in check had her wanting to break through that wall with a challenge.

"Because if you do think me capable of such deceptiveness, I shall tell you right now that I've had numerous opportunities to wed and have not accepted any of them."

An amused half-smile came with the reply to her challenge. "Much to the chagrin of those who love you."

Scowling, she demanded, "You will explain yourself, sir."

He started walking, forcing her to follow. "Perhaps I should start by saying how much I admire your father. And your many friends. They

45

care so much for you. Their devotion is astonishing."

"As is mine for them, but should one infer that you have no experience of this? That would be a shame."

"Miss Beatrice, I have many trusted friends but none would dare to interfere or step into my sphere. People know not to meddle with me and my affairs. They hesitate out of fear. The people who love you leap forward in your defense without any hesitation. I have observed that their protectiveness stems not only from affection. You are held in such high regard that no one wishes to cause you to think less of them. Your father has denied himself for some time out of dread that he might evoke disappointment on your part."

"Ridiculous. There is nothing about me that warrants such esteem." Then she gave serious thought to what he'd said. "Now you have me concerned. Did Father say that I have done him a disservice somehow?"

"He would never say so directly, but after witnessing his attentions to Mrs. Beardsley, it is my impression he has set aside his tender feelings for her."

"I don't understand your meaning, sir. Why would he deprive himself of her company?"

"So as not to give you the impression that you've lost precedence."

She started to scoff but intuition warned her to pay heed. She was in the company of a man unlikely to speak of personal issues to anyone, instigate problems for himself, or make himself the

46

catalyst in an uncomfortable state of affairs.

"Are you saying in a roundabout way that Father has set aside his interest in remarrying for my sake?"

"I may be incorrect, but that is my supposition. And please do not think me too forward in saying this, but when I asked for your hand, he appeared…relieved."

She stopped walking. They'd reached the end of the topiary. She stared blankly at the leafy green border wall, her brow wrinkled with a frown. "Relieved? How can that be? He told me how happy he was when I declined those offers."

An uneasy feeling slithered down her back when he inhaled a slow breath, as if preparing to say something dreadful.

She straightened her spine and demanded, "Tell me. I will have nothing less than the truth."

"Very well, Miss Beatrice, it shall be as you ask, unvarnished. Emily and Jonathan think so much of you and have long suffered concern for your future. I thought they would weep when I assured them that I was sincere about my offer. And truth be told, I hadn't expected your father to so readily agree to it. After I assured the Darcourts that it wasn't merely a ruse to circumvent Lady Richardson's vicious tongue, they revealed a curious tale of how everyone put forward an acceptable family member for you to marry."

"What? But why?"

"Apparently your father and the widow have been smelling of April and May for years. No one knew any other way to pry him free. Jonathan has offered him a comfortable retirement since your mother passed away."

She held up her hand. "Sir, do you imply that my father's parishioners have been plotting and arranging to get me married to someone, *anyone*, so that I will stop ruining his life?"

Instead of denying it, he looked her in the eye. "Beatrice, it's time to let him go."

Caught between humiliation and chagrin, she tightly asked, "Did the Darcourts say how many unfortunates were pressured to step forward?"

When he paused to rub the side of his nose in thought, she noticed a pronounced bump, not hooked-shaped, but a feature that suggested strength or belligerence. She suspected outright stubbornness when crossed.

"Not precisely," he said, bringing her back to the conversation, "but more than a few were encouraged to propose."

Disgusted, she admitted, "Well, counting you, six."

In silent agreement, they started walking again, heading back toward the topiary entrance. She tossed the twig she'd been carrying aside. "This is a dreadful mess. It must be sorted out somehow, and as I said before, I certainly have no intention of chivalrous expectations on your part."

"Perhaps I have a solution."

She suggested with ironic conviction, "Having Father start reading the banns this coming Sunday should *not* be a part of it."

"Hear me out. Emily raves about your writing skill beyond that which you do for your father. If I

48

understand this correctly, you're not scribbling novels in the privacy of your bower."

Unable to erase the sarcasm, she said, "No, Sir Jocelyn, I do not aspire to such depths."

He pursed his lips as if to hold in a thought or a smile. "Perhaps you could unbend enough to call me Joss until all is settled."

"I will consider it. What is your proposition?"

Chapter 6

Joss reviewed a rapid mental list of how he must present a potentially hazardous solution. He'd never been one for acting on sudden decisions, but in this case, he'd developed a fascination for this domineering, fiercely intelligent female.

Beatrice Allardyce tweaked his sense of humor— or as some of his friends had accused—a pronounced lack of one. He also admired her sincere sense of altruism. Her commitment to being of service came as naturally to her as breathing did for others. The other surprising upshot of meeting Miss Allardyce was an unexplained, almost obsessive yearning to be with her, or around her, relieved by the assurance of knowing exactly where she was. This immature or irrational yen to be in her company, being plagued by a feeling of unexplained longing, distracted and sapped his patience. The last few days since meeting her, he'd caught himself pacing while thinking about her. He briefly wondered if he were going off his head.

In any event, it was time for him to marry and this solved the dreary process of running to earth a spouse to carry on the line. Having latched on to the decision to land this pretty fish, he'd had to devise a bait too enticing for her to refuse out of hand.

"My proposition, as you call it, serves many purposes, for you and for me, but as in any negotiation, must supply incentives acceptable for all parties involved."

"A valid premise, sir. Please continue."

"Part one of my idea is to inform you that one of the many holdings that came to me with the baronetcy is a publishing concern. Do you aspire to publication?"

"Dreamt of it, sir, but I do not dwell on the improbable. I write and perfect it solely for my own pleasure."

"Then you have never seriously believed your works could be published?"

"One does have dreams but must also consider reality. It is my hope that in future publishers will come to their senses and judge a work by its merit and not by the gender of its writer."

"You might consider my company as a venue for your works."

Her reply contained equal parts of hopefulness and suspicion. "You cannot deem them worthy if you haven't read them."

"But I've *heard* how your mind works."

He looked away from the questioning expression that creased her brow, distracted by wisps of blond hair fluttering in the wind. It was best to stay fully engaged when dealing with Beatrice.

"You were saying, Sir Jocelyn?"

"Yes, the written word, specifically, yours. Your father quite readily admitted that you write his sermons. He also said that he rarely makes any corrections or changes. What is a sermon but an essay with a religious theme?"

"Well, yes, one could say that. What are the other parts of this proposition?"

"Only one other and that is we stay engaged. You

come to London. Stay with friends, or if you have family in town, and we'll go from there."

Discovering that she gaped, she snapped her mouth shut. After a tiny shake of her head, she asked, "Have you not taken into consideration that I am not interested in marriage, that I neither expect nor wish for you to sacrifice yourself for my sake?"

He paused to insert the monocle and study her as if inspecting a rare species, and she said, "Oh, do stop that appalling trick. I have no doubt it works very well for intimidating others, but I am not one of them."

He lifted his eyebrow, freeing the lens, and it tumbled down to dangle by its ribbon against his lapel. Pressing her lips into a dissatisfied moue, she stepped closer and righted it to lie flat. She also smoothed her gloved hand over the coat material, stopping mid-movement when she realized what she was doing.

Sounding out of breath, she mumbled an apology, stepped back, and started walking again at a brisk pace. Smiling, he followed.

"How kind of you Miss Allardyce. I don't believe anyone but my nurse and Cervantes have ever done me that kind service."

Continued breathlessness weakened her attempt to bolster a chastising reply. "Do not make fun of me, sir."

"Would never dream of it. I am quite sensible of your dignity and independent spirit."

"Who is Cervantes, other than the author."

"My valet. Returning to our original topic, may we agree that you wish to continue to write? You are determined on this goal. Correct?"

"I have come to that decision, yes, and am now utterly determined, even in the face of opposition from

52

every side."

"Indeed. It is a milieu comprised entirely of men with the exception of the few, odd novels, gothic tales mostly, for which you nourish a disdain. Correct?"

They came to a wooden stile and she accepted his hand to ascend the two steps. "That is correct." When he crossed over to join her on the other side, she turned to face him. "Your point, sir?"

"The point is your future. Your father will marry. I am sure the kind Widow Beardsley will welcome you as a daughter, but she, not you, will have the running of the house. Emily said that you have done so since the age of nine."

The tightening of her lips, the hastening of her step, let him know that this unhappy eventuality had already been given some thought. Beatrice Allardyce was a managing female. She couldn't help herself, poor dear. In most instances, this was a good and much appreciated thing, but living in the same roost where she'd dwelled and controlled, and where she would no longer rule, was a problem for someone so set in her ways. He knew this about her just as he had somehow known everything about her from the first.

Now that he had introduced the unpleasant truth, he brought up the heavy cannon, for this lady was no pushover. "My next point, if you will. Your father is not a young man. You came into the world later in the marriage of your parents. Not to put too fine a point on it, what are your prospects after his passing?"

She abruptly halted and squinted up at him, feathers fluffed for a fight. The defiance in her blue stare sent a thrill through his vitals that he'd have to think about later. For now, he had to keep his wits sharp and focused on the goal.

"You are rude, sir."

"No, I am blunt, but in fairness, you are not the first to voice that complaint."

"Then unkind."

"Is the truth unkind?"

He started walking again, knowing that she'd follow because she liked confrontation and argument and would pick up any gauntlet thrown down. "I am plain-speaking, hopefully never unkind. You inquired about my proposition. I'm merely laying down the platform for its conclusion. You did ask, did you not?"

"Sir Jocelyn, I will allow this conversation to continue to its end mainly because you are discussing the issue with the same attitude and respect you would with a male counterpart, but I will point out that you are taking a long time to come to its end."

"Then answer the previous, impolite question. What will you do when your father and stepmother have gone to their rewards?"

Her stubborn little chin lifted. "Seek employment."

"That response has so little confidence in its presentation that I should laugh. If I were indeed an *unkind* person."

"A point to be argued," she muttered.

He surprised himself with a rusty chuckle. "Perhaps later. And that laugh proves what my friends with truth aforethought complain when they say that I have no sense of humor. It seems I do when in your company."

"If our friends cannot be truthful with us, that would be a sad thing. It is your impression that my friends are loath to invoke my displeasure. That

54

concerns me a great deal."

"It shouldn't. You have an accessibility, a kind of reception of others that is rare. It's as if you observe but do not judge. That is more than rare."

He couldn't say out loud that she was loveable. He'd thought it was his imagination or his own affliction, but he'd witnessed how others were drawn to Beatrice no matter how ill-tempered or prickly her mood. She had a magnetic quality, an unconscious sensuality that was at the same time prim and alluring.

"That is very kind of you to point out, Sir Jocelyn."

"Very much in the purview of friendship, is it not? Even so, I digressed. Back to our subject."

"Your proposition."

"Yes. When I spoke with your father, his worry for your future was made clear. There are no relatives financially equipped to take an extra person into their households. Your dowry, if unused via marriage, amounts to scarcely enough for you to exist for a year. Should you become a governess, I have strong concerns that you might actually throttle an employer for their stupidity in the event some unsuspecting parent would hire you."

She stopped walking. "Now *that* is unkind."

"No, I am accurate. Do you expect me to believe that you would swallow the condescension and toads some ignorant matron forces on you?"

Her answer was to walk away. Fortunately, his legs were much longer. When he caught up with her, she veered and headed back toward Lowbridge Hall. He caught her arm to make her stop.

"Beatrice—"

"I did not give you leave, sir."

He tried not to let her apparent distress alter his course. "Very well, *Miss* Allardyce. You wouldn't be so angry were I not pointing out the obvious and in the right. I most heartily respect your writing pursuits, and yes, well aware that it makes me an oddity among my peers. On the other hand, most of them lack even a modicum of your intelligence. They are complacent about the serious social issues plaguing our country. Half of them sleep their way through Parliamentary sessions. Many of them take up positions without any consideration of facts, merely to side with whatever their friends find convenient or popular."

He caught himself expounding on an unrelated subject and quieted. She-who-misses-nothing eyed him with a crooked smile and said, "Now *you* sound angry."

"More like frustrated. I apologize for leaving the subject. My point is that the entirely unintentional event that threw us into a compromising situation may provide the opportunity to solve both of our problems."

"You *have* no problems, sir. You are financially sound according to Father. You live a life of freedom to indulge in sporting pursuits and do exactly as you please when you please. That is if one can believe your much vaunted racing and social successes printed in society sections. We do have newspapers here in the backwaters of England."

"Now you're off the subject."

"I am not, but do agree that I am intelligent."

"Then take into consideration that I am obligated to marry and continue the line."

"Surely there is someone to inherit?"

"Lands but not the title. The death of my brothers and years of war have left my family with no male inheritors. And Miss Allardyce, if I must spend the rest of my days tied to a culturally rendered illiterate, I will surely throttle someone."

"One would hope not your wife. And women of your station are known for their accomplishments."

"Ma'am, I do not consider a female accomplished merely because she can sew, produce inept watercolors and inappropriately spout studied phrases in Italian or French."

Looking down and away, she murmured, "I speak only dead and ancient languages."

Pleased with his progress, he suppressed a grin and teased with mock seriousness, "And yet there can be truth without copious amounts of wine."

She rewarded him with a gimlet eye and another half-smile. "And your friends say that you have no sense of humor. Very well, I will admit that I have an unacceptable abundance of pride that often doesn't allow me to bend or to give due patience to an opportunity."

He resisted the urge to crow, because he did love winning an argument. Deciding on which bait to employ, he tossed her the juiciest lure. "And what I propose is no gamble. All is ask is that you to take a moment to envision a life of abundance, one that affords you the time to write as long as you please, whatever you please, and most importantly of all, a venue for your work."

She halted, and with astonishment asked, "You could tell a publisher what to print?"

"When one holds the financial reins, Miss Allardyce, the direction is determined by the driver."

"A fitting simile for a Corinthian." With a

charming tilt of her head, she mulled over the tempting morsel he offered. And just like her, she dove directly into the subject's core by suspiciously asking, "Why do you offer this unparalleled opportunity to a female?"

He slowly reeled her into his net. "Why shouldn't women be afforded the same chance at fulfillment as men? We've written all of the books so far. Perhaps a feminine point of view will offer new perspectives."

"Very cleverly said, sir." She extended her hand. "I believe we have come to an understanding."

The grasp of her small hand in his was surprisingly strong. He bowed over it. "You have made me the happiest of men."

"I don't think it necessary to go that far. Respecting the truth and each other is enough to ask. You will let me know when you wish to start setting up the nursery."

She marched off in the direction of Lowbridge Hall and missed his victory grin. This time he did the gentlemanly thing at the stile by climbing the wooden steps ahead of her. He'd already gotten a glimpse of the delicacy of her ankles earlier, and now he noted the slenderness of her waist as he lifted her down, pretending to ignore the flutter of her eyelashes. Perhaps he should have employed flirtation rather than logic, then cast that idea aside when he likewise pretended to ignore her becoming blush. Timing had a great deal to do with the art of wooing and the craft of winning. Now wasn't the time for flirtation's game. Seduction was a strategy best utilized with spontaneity and when the outcome was assured. He'd already landed his prize and could afford to wait to indulge. The best angler knew how to draw in the caught fish without losing his catch. He'd lured her into agreeing to wed, and with the suggestion of a London visit, implanted the impression he was in no hurry to wed. While she grew accustomed to the idea of marriage, he would take care getting her safely inside his net.

Chapter 7

Joss went up the shallow steps to the knocker hanging on the shiny black entry to Asterly House. The mansion dominated Cavendish Square, a dwelling meant to impose, made of implacable granite, rows of sparkling windows, many chimneys and surrounded by formidable spikes of wrought iron fencing. A lackey at the door took his card, hat, gloves and cane. Since he had an appointment, he was led up to the first floor and down the passage to her ladyship's lair.

When he was announced, the woman behind the sprawling desk stood and came to greet him, both hands outstretched to take his in a firm grip. He nodded his head in a bow and smiled down at her handsome features and clever, hazel eyes.

"Thank you for seeing me, Lizzie, and on such short notice."

"Joss, it's good to have you back in town. Opening your house for the season?"

He nodded. "Came down early to get things in order. Is Peregrine at home?"

"He will be shortly. Would you care to move to a more comfortable room or speak here?"

"Here, if you please. I've always rather liked this room with its books and attempt to intimidate with that monstrous desk."

She chuckled, a sultry chortle that unintentionally

left many men weak-kneed. Lady Asterly never flirted. He liked that about her and the devious twistings of her mind. She was no one to cross and the best sort of friend, loyal and protective. Once you'd gained her trust, she had ways to make straight any path, ensure anyone's success, especially when it involved politics. Universally accepted as a female political wizard, she employed a man who knew everything about what was going on in London. If her wily butler, Crimm, didn't already know it, he would soon ferret out the secret.

She imitated affront with a pout. "Sir, you malign my desk. For that you shall have no tea."

"Just as well, because you know I prefer claret."

They sat in chairs situated by the windows to take advantage of watery sunlight and spoke of trivialities. After twenty minutes had passed and her husband hadn't presented himself, Lady Asterly gave him a level look and relaxed her smile into a serous expression.

"Joss, why have you come?"

He set his empty glass on the windowsill. "Advice. Direction. I had hoped to speak to Crimm."

"May I ask what about?"

"Lizzie, you could ask me for the moon."

Her lips curved in a sly smile. "I already have the moon. What do you need?"

"A publishing company."

She raised sable-brown eyebrows. "How unexpected. May I ask why?"

"I'm engaged, you see, and offered my intended carte blanche to publish her work. I may have alluded to owning a publishing business."

After pursing her mouth in thought, she asked,

"Are you quite sure about this? It could mean heartache instead of validation."

"How kind of you to approach it that way, but she is quite intelligent and I believe, gifted."

"This is not an infatuation speaking, is it, Joss?"

"Could be, but perhaps I can encourage her to use a male nom de plume to save her from distress."

"Encourage? Oh, Joss, this is indeed amusing. I shall leap ahead and assume that this marriage is nothing contracted to a marriage mart girl just out."

"You know me better than that, Lizzie."

Again, her appealing chuckle made him wary. "Oh, this is *too* delicious. The grand and unapproachable Sir Jocelyn brought low by a smart girl. She must have made a remarkable first impression."

The memory of her waving derriere stuck between the fence boards bloomed. "One could say that. So, Lizzie, what do you advise? May I ask Crimm to locate a company for sale or a firm open to taking on a partner?"

"First, I must ask a question, because this is just too entertaining to pass by. You are telling me that you secured the attentions of your intended by promising her publication with a company that you do not already own, but you told her that you do?"

"May I have another glass of wine?"

"No. Admit it, Joss, and quit trying to hide the fact that you are squirming inside."

"Lady Asterly, I come to you for aid and you torture me?"

The door opened and Major Lord Asterly swung through the opening. He went directly to his wife, leaned down, and kissed her, completely without

62

hesitation or consideration that there was a visitor present.

Robust, his sandy hair starting to silver, and built like the soldier he was, Asterly grinned and propped his elbow on the back of his wife's chair. "How goes it, Joss? Ready for sessions to open?"

Before he could reply, Lizzie spoke up. "He's affianced, Peregrine, to a girl smarter than he is! She got him to promise to publish her novel."

Joss held up his hand. "That needs correcting immediately. Not a novel! Heaven forbid. Beatrice Allardyce considers novel writing beneath her. She's an essayist, poor thing. We all know no one will listen to a female writing, much less an essayist."

Asterly shrugged a shoulder. "I don't know that it should be that difficult. Prinny adores Miss Austen, but Joss, I never knew you owned a publishing house or had connections with one."

Lizzie laughed. "And there's the rub! He *doesn't*. He must talk some publisher into printing her essay or find a business who is open to partnership!"

Asterly shook his head and leaned forward to flick his wife's nose. "You terrible creature. You didn't tell him that you own one. Joss, I bet if you asked nicely, my Lizzie would let you invest."

Joss scowled. "Lady Asterly, you hung me up to dangle on the noose, while the entire time you planned to help me out?"

She grinned and stood. "You deserved a bit of roasting after leading that girl on with a promise that you might not be able to keep."

Joss stood with her. "Oh, I definitely would have kept it. Miss Beatrice Allardyce will have it no other

63

way. But I must warn you, she speaks her mind and hasn't much interest in politics."

Asterly slid a hand around his wife's waist and drew her close to his side as they strolled to the door. Their open affection was uncommon, but somehow accepted in a society that considered such public displays gauche. Viewing it, and their easy fondness for each other, evoked an odd twisting just under his heart. He attributed it to the spicy lamb stew he'd had the night before and not bothering with breakfast this morning.

Lizzie stopped him at the door with a pat on his arm. "Not to worry, Joss. I won't make a liar out of you. Have your secretary speak with my trustees. They'll arrange for an investment clause. Let them know how much you wish to invest. I'll let the publishers know you have carte blanche. And Joss, I must meet your Miss Allardyce the minute you bring her to town."

He wryly said, "I have yet to pin her down for a wedding date."

Asterly shared a speaking gaze with his wife, and didn't break eye contact with her as he said, "I suggest training her in the way she should go, especially when it comes to learning how to get your way, like this one does. She dangles the sweet and vows it can't be eaten until she gets exactly what she wants."

Joss answered, "Not sure that will work with Beatrice but more than willing to give it a try. It's not easy to stay a step ahead of her. What is the name of the publishing company?"

"Lockerby and Sunderland," Lizzie answered, pulling her gaze from her husband's. "Make it a fait accompli. Tell them I sent you, and they will shortly be receiving a submission from you, which they will print at the earliest opportunity. Then go marry your clever girl, Joss. I'm agog to meet the female who can hold your interest for more than five minutes."

"I feel I should warn you. My intended is not in the order of your typical country mouse."

Asterly waggled his eyebrows. "Did you hear that, Lizzie. She bites."

His wife swatted his arm. "Behave, Asterly. Ignore him, Joss. He's incorrigible. You are not to worry. Do be assured that I prefer people of stout character. It's said that the atheist is easier to turn than the agnostic."

Joss smiled but felt some concern that his intended might be more than they expected. He vividly recalled how she hadn't budged when he'd taken that half-trained hunter of Jonathan's over the rock wall and directly at her. Beatrice had stood her ground, while Emily cowered behind her friend's back. He'd known he could bring the horse to a halt, but an onlooker would not. His stubborn Bea refused be intimidated. Perhaps he should be more concerned about the people she would meet when he lured her to town. He'd never encountered anyone so utterly uninterested in making an impression.

Being a gentleman of good birth and income, his place in society was assured, but Beatrice Allardyce lived by her own standard. He'd never heard her make judgments on others with the exception of himself, which was perplexing. He had enjoyed a brief fling with sporting and social pursuits after he'd been given the financial means to do so. Curricle racing, card playing and gaming were expected. He'd never

65

overindulged. Well, there were a few occasions that gave rise to gossip, but after learning his lessons, he'd leveled out. He couldn't see how she could set him down as a hardened gamester now, or as she'd called him, a buck about town. First impressions were everything to some. He'd been in an impatient mood as he'd walked through the village and had come upon Mrs. Pritchard's cottage.

Remembering how he'd halted mid-stride from the sight of Beatrice caught in the fence, he silently laughed. Life would never be dull with her sharp tongue and sharper mind. His problem would be staying a mental step ahead.

Chapter 8

Beatrice admired the teacup's floral design as she set her empty cup on the tray. One of the joys of spending time with Emily at Lowbridge Hall was the excellence of the tea and the talents of her cook. The aroma of freshly baked pastries hung in the air.

Exhaling a contented sigh, Beatrice leaned back against the Egyptian motif couch. "I should be as fat as a grouse if I lived here at Lowbridge. How do you and Jonathan stay so slim?"

"Delicacies like these are especially made when you are here. When Mrs. Bellavent hears that you are to visit, she bakes like it's the return of the prodigal son."

Beatrice finished the tea in her cup and set it on the tray. "I don't know why I should be afforded so much courtesy but very much appreciate it. The raspberry jam is divine."

When Beatrice declined more tea, Emily refreshed her own cup. "How could you have forgotten or give so little credit for what you did for her son?"

Beatrice waved her hand. "It was nothing."

"Nothing? He had measles and you risked your life caring for him and all of us. The entire house was quarantined and you breezed through the door and took charge like a field marshal."

"What have you heard from your cousin Alice?"

Emily frowned and shook her head. "Beatrice, that is *not* what I expected you to ask. You know very well that we must talk about your wedding ceremony."

67

When Beatrice pretended interest in the couch seat's slick material, gliding her palm over golden satin, Emily persisted, "The third of the banns were read last Sunday. You must give some thought as to what you will wear, the preparation of a trousseau. Why, you haven't asked about where you'll live. Joss has five houses. One in London is situated near Hyde, but my favorite is a neat little—"

"I may not go through with it."

Emily stared, slack-jawed, then whispered, "What? Beatrice, you can't mean to *jilt* him?"

Tilting her chin at a belligerent angle, she replied, "I'm considering it."

"Oh, Beatrice. You mustn't even think it! That horrid Lady Richardson will have everything she's said about you made to sound true. You aren't fast. Good heavens, if anything, the opposite."

"What do I care about her gossip? Or anything said about me for that matter. Life is littered with more important issues and difficulties than a bored woman's trivial remarks."

"But it could ruin you when you go to London."

Unable to moderate escalating impatience, she shot back, "But I'm not *going* to London, Emily."

They were interrupted by the opening of the drawing room door. A footman announced, "Sir Jocelyn Warfield."

"Of course it is," Beatrice muttered as she stood with Emily, who immediately flew to greet him.

"Joss, we didn't expect you until tomorrow."

"I apologize for the inconvenience, Emily, and for coming to you in all my dirt. Just arrived you can see and heard that Miss Allardyce was here."

Beatrice dipped a sullen courtesy and was further annoyed when he grinned at her insolence. "Not in a happy mood, are we, Miss Allardyce?"

"Not at present," she said to the floor.

"Perhaps a walk would restore your spirits. If you do not mind, Emily?"

Her traitorous, matchmaking friend beamed her delight. "Certainly not. We keep country hours, you know, but there is still plenty of time before dinner."

He nodded his head in a bow. "If you'll excuse me, I'll come down to fetch Miss Allardyce after Cervantes makes me presentable."

Beatrice glared at the closed door. "Makes himself presentable? Gracious, this isn't a London salon, and he looks neat as a pin."

With a smug grin, Emily sashayed to the couch and tugged Beatrice down to sit beside her. "He has manners, Bea! You can't fault him for that. He's everything I would ever want for you." Her expression settled into sadness, her brown eyes worried. "Beatrice, you must make yourself content with this most advantageous arrangement. Be sensible. What else can you do? Your father and Mrs. Beardsley are to be married this Saturday. You know how it goes after that and you know yourself. You will feel in the way and at loose ends without a house to run."

"But who will see to the vestments? Setting flowers out on Sunday and helping at Evensong? There are parishioners to see to and sermons to—"

"Bea, dearest, your father has retired. The new pastor will arrive in time for the ceremony. His wife will take care of all of the things you've been doing for years. Now is the time for careful consideration of *your* future. If not marriage, where will you go, and what will you do with your life? Your father and new mother would never turn you out, and you are always welcome here, but you are meant for so much more than living for this parish."

Assaulted by a sudden dose of cold reality, Beatrice gripped her friend's hand, confessing in a small, unfamiliar voice, "Oh, Em, I never thought I'd get married. What I have for a dowry is laughable. I am no great beauty and no longer a girl. I do know how to run a house, but what could any man find interesting about me? And I am too educated."

Emily pulled her hand free and wrapped her arms around Beatrice's slumped shoulders. "But you are exactly what Joss needs. He would go mad around the girl society thinks of as perfect. I've never understood why he's so patient with me and Jonathan."

Beatrice leaned back from the embrace, swiped away a tear. With a playful scowl she teased, "*Stoopid*. You're both appallingly adorable."

Their giggling fit was interrupted when the door opened and Joss stepped through. He held Beatrice's bonnet and a fringed shawl. After tying the bonnet ribbons, she allowed him to drape the shawl around her shoulders. She kissed Emily's cheek and accepted Joss's arm.

As they went down the steps and strolled toward the alley of ancient oaks that guarded the lane to the house, she asked, "How often do you change clothes in a day?"

"That would depend on where I am, the appointments or events. How often do you?"

"This is the country, sir. One doesn't need to
70

change one's clothes when one already looks immaculate. There was scarcely a wrinkle on you and you'd come all the way from London."

"There are particular standards one must maintain, and it is necessary to keep Cervantes occupied. Otherwise he would be bored, and one doesn't wish to have one's servants embarrassed by their employers."

"He sounds like a tyrant."

"Of course he is. He's my valet. He maketh the man, not necessarily manners."

"The Winchester motto? Did you attend there?"

"Yes and later to Oxford. My brothers were alive then and I was meant for the clergy."

"Would you have liked that?"

"I believe I would have been content. You aren't having second thoughts, are you?"

She didn't respond immediately and was relieved when he waited for her answer. "I must be honest. Emily and I were discussing that very subject when you arrived. I'd planned my life, you see, never thinking to marry."

"You never wanted children?"

She countered with, "Do you, other than being obliged to carry on the title?"

"I'd always thought it would be nice to have a sister. There are mostly boys in my family. A girl would be nice, but you shouldn't think that children would take away from your writing. During childhood, I rarely saw my parents and didn't converse with my father until after I'd left university."

"You were not close to him?"

"No and certainly not in the way of you and your father. Your relationship with him is quite enviable. My father maintained strict beliefs about children being reared by nurses and tutors until of an age to not be an embarrassment at dinner and in adult company."

"I know that is the way of things among the Upper Ten, but shouldn't like that sort of life for my children. I spent all of my time with my father and can't imagine not interacting with my own child."

"I have no reference for that sort of parenting. Father always kept himself at a distance, even after adulthood, but it will be exactly as you wish. I don't care as long as the line continues, but I might be disappointed not to have a girl."

They walked in silence for a while, she finding it impossible to imagine him spoiling and doting on a daughter. Everything about him was austere and exacting, somehow aloof and yet not in a manner that was off-putting. She again envisioned him in that relaxed pose, shirt undone, a lazy-eyed expression, and shivered.

"Are you cold?" he asked.

She withdrew her hand from the crook of his arm to adjust the shawl. "No. I was thinking about how our personalities and situations differ."

"Not by very much. Let us first address any concerns you may have." He retrieved her hand and tucked it back where it had been as they resumed walking. "Is there anything you wish to confide? Any questions about our getting married? I would like to set your mind at rest."

"Well, to be frank, I do have qualms when it comes to acting as hostess in a political setting. My education is academic, not political. Running a household is a mundane, a simple matter of knowing how to balance a budget and suppling what is needed for everything to run smoothly. But I am not confident I could be the informed and polished hostess you would wish. I have absolutely no artistic talents, nothing in the way of what is considered feminine skills, no interest in political thought. How could I carry on a discussion? And why do you smile?"

"Because accomplishing what you're unsure about is so very simple. All that is required is to limit your access to the wine decanter."

She grumbled, "Will I *ever* live that incident down?"

"In all seriousness, it's quite easy. When conversing with a politician, all one has to do is listen and pretend to agree, then go about thinking exactly as one likes. Everyone will set you down as impossibly brilliant. Believe me, he'll be so impressed with himself, he will never know that you think he's an imbecile."

"You are too cynical, sir"

"And that brings to mind another thing. A concern you might not wish to air but one that must be laid to final rest. I fully understand your dream, your compulsion, if you will, to create with words, and will never stand in your way. I also have this within me, in my own, small way, of course. Nothing in line of your talents."

"What a happy coincidence! What discipline? History or ethics of politics?"

"Nothing so challenging, Miss Beatrice. I never did tell you that yours is a name I've always liked. Why, that's a lovely blush you're wearing. I shall have to think up ways to make you do that more often."

"Please, don't. I'm not accustomed to flirting."

"Strangely enough, neither am I. But I am glad it is decided between us and that you are content that I shall be your Benedick. To answer your previous question, my interest lies in poetry."

She pounced on the opportunity to move the topic away from two famous lovers. "Ah, poetry! Will you share some of your creative endeavors with one who will be gentle with an artist's tender sensibilities?"

When he demurred, she squeezed his arm and encouraged, "It need not be extemporaneous, sir. Perhaps some idea or verse in progress?" When he again showed reluctance, she added, "Speaking out loud what you have written helps with revision and correction."

"Very well, since you have promised to be kind to an amateur."

He stepped away from her hold and clasped his hands behind his back as they strolled down the tree-shaded alley. She remained respectfully silent and patient as he prepared. For her, this was a holy moment, this finding the courage in oneself and giving voice to one's creation. She waited, not daring to interfere, feeling like a vessel to be filled with the shared joy of inspiration. As he watched the passage of his boots along the lane, his lowered voice sounded halting and pensive.

"When I have seen the hungry ocean gain advantage on the kingdom of the shore, and firm soil win of the watery main, increasing store with...loss, and loss with store."

He paused and she waited, projecting in her silence solemn interest to hear what would follow. He gently cleared his throat and squinted up at the sky before he continued.

"When I have seen such interchange of state, or state itself confounded to decay, ruin teaches me to ruminate that time will come and take my love away…and this thought is as a death…which cannot choose…but to weep to have that which it fears to lose."

She halted to stare up at him, eyes wide, her mouth open in an *oh* of awe. "Why, sir, you see me profoundly impressed! That is formidable verse indeed."

After he humbly tipped his head to acknowledge her praise, she continued walking, sagely nodding as she critiqued, "I must confess that I am prodigiously moved as well. And as impressed hearing you recite those marvelous couplets, as I was when I first read them in a book of sonnets by Shakespeare. I believe you paraphrased, did you not?"

His stony expression wavered, then cracked when he laughed. "Caught me out, old girl. Well done! Is there anything you haven't read?"

"Oh, a great deal. Father's library is limited. Financial constraints, you understand. The living for a country parson doesn't lend itself to the acquisition of books, but I am fortunate in that I can pilfer from the library at Lowbridge. Is that a favorite sonnet?"

"Of my mother's. She liked having it read to her."

He offered his arm again and she took it. He placed his hand over hers as he said, "Please don't consider this an impertinence, but I can't imagine that Jonathan would deny your father or his parish priest anything."

"In the first place, Father would never ask for an

increase, and you are entirely correct in that the Darcourts furnish an extremely generous stipend. I wouldn't want you to think otherwise of your friend and mine."

"But then—"

When he left the thought hanging, she explained, "We have plenty for our needs, but there are others in the shire not so fortunate. It is our pleasure, Father's and mine, to share. Please don't tell him that I've divulged this. He would be mortified."

"I will honor that. Now, how can I phrase what I would like to ask you?"

"However you wish, sir. I am not a frail reed, if you haven't already noticed."

"Beatrice, one cannot fail to notice that you're always taking care of others. Who takes care of you?"

She stopped, her expression startled. Appalled when tears welled up in her eyes, he grasped her hands. "I never meant to overset you. Forgive me. I thought it an innocent enough question."

Blinking away the tears, she swiped the wet from her cheeks and inhaled a shaky breath. "No, you must forgive me. One wouldn't wish to appear maudlin."

"Or sentimental." With a rueful grin, he squeezed her hands. "I do beg your pardon, but have you never noticed that? How you are constantly serving others and nothing much is done for you? Beatrice, from all I've noticed, you even make do without adequate staff and a personal maid."

She tried to withdraw from his grasp, but he wouldn't let go. "That moment of weakness had nothing to do with self-pity, and the lack of personal maid a matter of choice."

He leaned down to peek under her bonnet brim. "Beatrice, you mustn't take everything I say as some form of accusation. I was merely making a point to secure your faith in your decision for us to wed."

"You never make an argument with only one point."

"Most astute of you. The caveat is that marriage means that you not only have time to pursue your vocation but also ample funds for charities of your choosing. Ah, I see that point may have turned the tide."

"Your determination knows no boundary, sir. I should have known from the first with that nose of yours."

In an obvious effort to put the previous awkwardness behind them, he teased, "And look who is taking about hawkish noses. You probably have no idea of this, but you have a slight curve to yours."

"Sir, do you have the effrontery to suggest that I am a hook-nose? Not very gentlemanly of you, and neither is laughing at my indignation."

"Silly Bea, it isn't in the least hooked."

"Trying to save face, are you? Well, I shan't let you off this particular hook, and you're a fine one to tease with that nose of yours."

"Truly hooked, is it?"

"Not really, no, but there is a bump that makes your profile decidedly formidable."

"Ah, then we must resolve ourselves to our offspring appearing unfortunately hawkish." He stopped walking when she halted. He searched her face then took both of her fisted hands in his. "Beatrice, please, you mustn't worry about that. There's no immediate need for us to start setting up our nursery. As you have said, marriage was never an expectation for you. That part can happen when the time is convenient and amenable to both. Does that sound agreeable?"

Her stiffened shoulders relaxed. "Actually, it sounds quite agreeable. There is a certain mindset to that, you know."

He patted her hand before replacing it on his arm. "I am fully sensible of the delicacy of that matter. Indeed, you must feel that we have rushed this particular fence. There is nothing wrong with taking time to get to know one another. And for you to meet my friends. I am sure Lady Asterly and Lady Collyns can steer you onto the right course. They have their fingers in many charitable pies, any number of good works. There will be plenty for you to do in London."

"I'm rather a country girl, you know."

"Which is why I haven't done much with the house in town and opened the Willows."

"Willows? Another house outside of London? But won't that make things difficult for you?"

"No. It's not that far from town. Willows is a more countrified setting where I believe you will feel more comfortable. Then what say you to having your father marrying us after the final banns are read on Sunday? Come on, old girl. Let's get it done and out of the way, give your father and the new Mrs. Allardyce privacy."

When she stopped again, he said, "Beatrice, I am not taking control of your life. I'm giving you the means to control yours."

"But men have all the power once a woman marries."

78

"And before, if we're about to get accurate with the way of things. But this Benedick wants his Beatrice to have her freedom."

"I imagine they all say that before throwing the net over one's head," she muttered.

He held up his hands. "See? No net."

She replied to that with a hum of cynicism and headed back to Lowbridge. "Time will tell."

Chapter 9

The day after their wedding, Joss sat beside her on the forward seat. Beatrice pulled her gaze from the view outside the chaise, when he asked, "Do you feel differently now that you are married?"

His constant proximity continued to disturb. She'd assumed that she would become accustomed to his sitting so near, but the unsettling nervousness hadn't faded. His question was a welcomed distraction.

She'd been reviewing their brief wedding; the joy on her father's face, Emily and Jonathan beaming their approval, the scent of lavender when Mrs. Beardsley, now Mrs. Allardyce, pressed a cool cheek to her own. It had been a pleasant, brief ceremony, almost anticlimactic. After a light luncheon at the coaching inn, she and Joss were on the road to London, away from the only place she'd lived her entire life.

She looked away from the countryside and down at her gloved hands clenched on her lap. "Not really. Odd, isn't it? One would think the world would seem entirely different after such a life altering event."

When she lifted the backs of her fingers to her mouth to stifle a yawn, he asked, "Did you sleep well?"

"Very well, thank you. The bed wasn't damp and the sheets were clean."

A smile ticked up one corner of his mouth. "Yes, that would be the case. While we had dinner, Cervantes saw to our rooms and baggage. Did the maid the inn provided prove acceptable?"

80

"Of course. I didn't see your manservant. I'm beginning to think he's imaginary."

"He drove ahead in the curricle to make arrangements at the inn. Could we perhaps manage to find something less boring to talk about?"

"Ah, but I was on the cusp of pointing out something quite mundane."

"You could never be."

"You may wish to change that opinion, because I meant to comment that this is a very nice carriage for a rented vehicle. Now I must think of something interesting, beyond how one must appreciate the smoother ride."

"Or we could continue with the inconsequential and you could point out that Hampshire keeps the roads well-graded."

She scoured her mind for topics, but it remained barren. The oddness, the something intangible about his closeness, kept intruding, making her thoughts scatter. The constant warmth and disconcerting hardness of his thigh against her own made it impossible to think clearly. As the hours passed, she'd been forced to resort to staring out the window, even when rain obscured the view.

Happily, a thought came to mind and she seized it. "For my part, I'm relieved to be out of Hampshire. It has so many reputed robberies. We have a neighbor who insisted that she would never recover after being robbed of her purse and jewelry on the infamous Heath. I have very little in the way of possessions or money, but had I anything of worth, I would never keep it in my purse or jewelry on my person. I would tuck it in a pouch and hide it between the seat cushions."

"A sensible idea but one would think that any thief worth his mettle would make a search of possible hiding areas."

A bit deflated, she murmured, "Yes, I suppose he would. And here I thought myself so clever."

He placed a large, gloved hand over hers. "Are you anxious?"

She looked out the window where the rain was letting up, revealing a cleanly washed landscape. "Mayhap a little apprehensive. A new life, you know. Then there is the possibility of robbery at pistol-point."

"There's no need to worry about that."

He leaned forward and pulled out a narrow drawer underneath the opposite seat. She felt her eyes widen at the sight of a pistol.

"Is it loaded?" she asked when he left it there and pushed the drawer shut.

"It wouldn't be as effective were it not. Highwaymen appear suddenly I've been told. It would take too long to prime and load."

"I see." She dared a glance at him and encountered his hooded observation, increasing the apprehension she couldn't conceal. "Is that why you sit on this side? For the clearer view of where you think a highwayman might appear?"

"Partly, but yes."

"And you'd…shoot him?"

The monocle dropped from his eye when he quirked a dark eyebrow. "That is precisely why the pistol is kept within reach."

"Ah, I see. I doubt that I could bring myself to do that. Money, jewels, such possessions should never be given the importance of a human life."

82

"That depends on one's estimation of what is valuable."

Glad to argue, she readied to contradict him. "Jewels can be replaced. According to Father, you have plenty of money. I cannot imagine a possession so dear that it is irreplaceable." His smile, rather chilling, and his unblinking stare stopped her from arguing further.

"I agree with you in part but not in the whole. You might not pull a trigger but you would never tolerate the ill-treatment of a weaker being. And you've forgotten what any right thinking husband would consider as irreplaceable."

When she said nothing, caught in his gaze, he said, "You."

In that moment, more than any other in his company, she sensed his maleness. His touch always evoked a suggestion of strength and curious undercurrent within her body. Whenever she took his hand to step down from the coach or up a step, she sensed about him a virile dominance restrained. She'd noticed it first while walking with him at Lowbridge, when he lifted her down from the style. There had been the insinuation of something suppressed, quiet, bidding its time.

She pulled her attention away from his level regard, unsettled by a brief spark in his gaze and its quicker disappearance. She pretended interest in the passing view. "How long before we get to Willows?"

"Late afternoon. I'm relieved you slept well. The taproom remained noisome into the night. Some sort of local celebration. You will rest easier at Willows."

"Yes. The uproar below stairs did make it feel as if I weren't alone in my bed."

A flush of heat rose up her neck and crept into her face. One might interpret her off hand remark with another nuance. Would he misconstrue her meaning and think she wished to start the physical side of marriage without delay?

She gave her head a tiny shake to cast off the discomfort. She was acting too sensitive. Over thinking everything. But perhaps not, since he immediately began a one-sided conversation on another topic. After she got her thoughts and body under control she was able to converse rationally. She tried not to calculate why she was acting so strangely. Thank goodness that very soon they would no longer be in such close proximity.

When they stopped for the last change of horses, she declined luncheon, which pleased Joss. He confessed to his preference for faster travel and would rather be on the road as soon as possible. She assured him that she had no objections to speed.

Before they reentered the coach, she waited while he told the coachman to pick up the pace for the last leg of the journey. A groom had been following them on the headstrong hunter he'd bought from Jonathan, and she encouraged Joss to ride rather than sit inside with her. He startled her when he gave her a broad smile and a peck on the cheek before telling the groom to take a seat up on the box.

Outside the chaise window, Joss kept pace with the loping team. With a touch of his hat brim and a nod, he let her know that he was riding ahead. Then he leaned forward and the gelding lunged forward out of view. She glimpsed his pleasure as he freed the horse to run, bringing back the recollection of him taking the high-

84

strung chestnut over the rock wall at Lowbridge. So wild and reckless, like his famed racing exploits. How different he was from her first impression of him, which had been one of supreme urbanity, holding himself aloof and above common folk. There had been no indication of wildness under the façade. How did he keep so much passion and ferocity concealed? A quiver sizzled up her arms and down her spine. Perhaps she should have taken the time to uncover what resided beneath the veneer before marrying him.

Chapter 10

When the chaise slowed to stop, Beatrice leaned forward for her first impression of Willows. Built of the red brick that was popular during the Renaissance, the sixteenth century country house stood back from the main road, protected by larch, oaks, and a lane of tall rhododendrons. A broad swath of neatly rolled lawns surrounded the three-storied house. The stable block, carriage house, and other outbuildings were partially hidden behind hedgerows and trees.

When she took Joss's hand to step down onto the gravel drive, he asked, "Do you like it?"

"You know I do. To be frank, I never expected anything so charming. And peaceful."

"Too bucolic for my father, but Mother loved it here." He took her arm as they walked toward the entry.

Household staff waited inside, since clouds had gathered, darkening the sky. A freshening breeze spat stinging droplets, hurrying them indoors. After she'd been greeted and introduced to the heads of staff, Joss escorted her upstairs. A wide central staircase separated the first floor wings, leading up to a spacious, airy landing that had broad passages in three directions.

He took her arm as they moved down the center corridor. "Our rooms are directly ahead. Situated for the best views of the river, of course. These are yours. The sitting room first."

He pushed open a door and she paused just beyond
86

the doorway. "Oh, my word."

She felt him watching as she glanced around the light-washed room. Walls of the palest green had been etched with vines and lavender flowers. The ceiling was a bower of twining colors and frolicking deer. A writing desk had been placed before a wide window that looked out on the river. She crossed to it immediately, noticing the softness underfoot of a green-and-pink patterned Aubusson carpet. Beyond the mullioned panes, the lawn slanted gracefully downward to the river's edge, where heavy-headed willows swayed in the rising breeze.

She sensed his presence approaching, his intensity soaking into her back when he halted behind her. "I had the desk brought over here by the windows and Mother's chaise moved closer to the fire. It can get damp, being so near to the river. Of course, you will arrange the rooms as you like. Mine are through there."

He pointed at a dressing room door ajar and the adjacent master bedroom. Movements within showed servants busy with trunks and baggage. Hers were being brought in and carried through to a bedchamber connected to the sitting room. A young woman, dark-eyed and dusky-haired directed the footmen carrying her trunk and bandboxes. Compared to Joss's traveling luggage, hers seemed pitifully sparse.

Joss gestured and the young woman approached, halting with a curtsey, keeping her gaze on the floor as he introduced, "This is Carter. She was suggested until you decide on a personal maid."

After Beatrice nodded, Carter went back to directing the footmen, while Joss took her arm. "If you would wait here a moment, I should like to introduce

87

you to Cervantes and Evans."

He called and a slim, elegant man stepped through from the master bedroom. "Yes, sir?"

"Evans, this is Lady Warfield. Leave the correspondence for now. We can see to it after dinner. We've traveled a long way today and will be retiring early. If you would, have my schedule for tomorrow ready. I will look at the most pressing of commitments in the morning. Would you send in Cervantes?"

As the secretary left, Joss said, "I apologize for that bit of tedious business, but I've let many things slide recently. Something important must have brought Evans upstairs. Something that can't wait."

"How may I be of service, sir?" a deep, rolling voice interrupted.

"Ah, Cervantes, this is Lady Warfield. Make sure all of her luggage is taken from the chaise. There is a red leather bandbox that must be found and brought up. Put it by the desk."

The blond giant bowed and stepped back, disappearing into the dressing room and swiftly through to the master bedroom. Blinking at his retreating figure, she asked, "*That* is Cervantes?"

"Now you know why I'm ever eager to hop to his command."

"If that smirk you're wearing is any indication, I beg leave to give you the opinion that you're not in the least afraid of him. But one could certainly see why one might be. He looks every inch the marauding Viking. Is Cervantes his real name?"

"Of course not. And we shall leave it at that. Have a rest and I'll have dinner brought up whenever you like. Or would you prefer a walk down by the river?

The rain has moved off. The grass will be wet."

"I adore walking on wet grass with no shoes, and a walk does sound refreshing, but I'm tired. Would you mind waiting for another time?"

"Not at all. Let Carter know when you're ready for dinner. We can have it set up in here if you like."

She smiled. "How kind and considerate."

With a sardonic twist on his lips, he nodded a bow. "Quite the husbandly prerogative, don't you think?"

She pulled a face. "Don't ruin it, sir."

He silently laughed as he left. She turned back to the view, unable to believe that she'd stepped into a fairyland. Willows was a haven sublime, better than anything she'd ever imagined what life would be like confined in a marriage. It was an adjustment, coming to the understanding that she now had ample time to write without interruption, any time she wished, even long into the night. The responsibilities she had embraced— and lamented only to herself—began to fade from worry into acceptance. The confusing lack of everyday tasks and obligations, the habitual busyness of her former life, was beginning to feel less like an unsettling absence and more like a blessed relief.

She pivoted to respond to a tap on the bedroom door, but Carter came swiftly through from the bedroom to answer it. She stepped back to allow Cervantes to enter. He had the bandbox crammed with her writing materials propped on a shoulder.

"Where, my lady?"

Beatrice gestured to a chair by the desk. "Place it across the chair arms, please."

"Would you like it opened, my lady?"

"No, Cervantes. Thank you."

She watched him leave, a great, hulking figure who moved with fluid athletic grace. She fancied he would look more appropriately dressed in mail and helm rather than form-fitting frock coat and the immaculate linen of a gentleman's gentleman.

On the desk, an envelope made of expensive vellum stood propped against a Dresden figurine of a shepherdess and a lamb. It was addressed to Lady Warfield. As uncomfortable as it yet was to accept the name as her own, she took up the letter and broke the seal.

An invitation from Lord and Lady Asterly, who would be pleased to make their acquaintance as soon as it proved agreeable. In addition, if she wished, she could chose any day she liked for a small gathering of artists, writers and friends to celebrate their nuptial with a musical evening.

She tapped the edge of the card against her lower lip. It was one thing to muddle through an evening without the reprieve of comfortable conversation. Over the years, she'd become accustomed to that, since all she could talk about in polite society was books. Only men read what she read, and they blanched whenever she introduced academic topics, or they turned up avuncular, which bothered her more than their condescension.

Perhaps a bit about philosophy might squeak through in a pinch, but her social skills could only be deemed abysmal. As for social accomplishments, she could stumble her way through a few bars of an etude on the pianoforte, had no training with any other instrument, had no great interest in art, and a singing voice that was merely passable when it came to hymns during service. She had so little to recommend her as suitable spouse to one such as Sir Jocelyn.

Emily and Jonathan had raved about the social successes of Lady Asterly's gatherings, salons that rivaled French society at the height of Paris revelry. Joss would expect her to look presentable. The blue satin she'd worn for the dinner disaster that got her married to him would have to do until more could be purchased.

Perhaps Lady Asterly would condescend to advise. The village seamstress and her own finishing touches had been good enough for the country but would never do for the *beau monde*. Conforming to fashion was one thing. Stopping the constant activity of her mind and the words that made a fast track from her brain to flying out of her mouth was another.

However does one go about learning to dissemble? Was all this fuss worth it for a home of her own, having her written views and opinions aired, the insignificance of her reputation upheld? She'd told Emily that she didn't care what the world thought of her, and that was the truth, but one wouldn't wish to render one's spouse a laughingstock.

Ah, well, perhaps no one would notice the stocking she'd have to cram into her mouth to keep her thoughts to herself.

Chapter 11

Joss was resolute about making a call to introduce her to Lord and Lady Asterly as soon as possible. They did so on a day other than her ladyship's proscribed at home day, proof of the closeness of her husband's friendship with the Asterlys.

The imposing granite, four-story, many-windowed mansion in Cavendish Square didn't intimidate. Joss's admiration of Lady Asterly did. The ton's distinguished arbiters, like the Ladies Cowper, Castlereagh and Jersey, accepted but didn't encourage the baron's wife, whose father had been in trade. She was placed on a par with the Whig political hostess, Lady Melbourne and held well above the divorced Lady Holland.

From Joss she'd learned that Elizabeth Asterly did the unthinkable; she managed her own and her husband's accounts. Prior to their marriage, she maneuvered the financial strings of her vast wealth through a pair of trustees. Once married to the baron, he turned everything over to her to be done in his name. From this information and Joss's high regard, Beatrice understood that the woman she was about to meet was distinguished by him as something more than merely extraordinary.

After introduction to this paragon, Beatrice felt somewhat silly. Her imagination had her expecting a great beauty or dauntingly modish matron. Lady Asterly looked in no way unusual. She was what one described as handsome with an understated elegance in her style and sharp acumen gleaming in too-perceptive hazel eyes.

Major Lord Asterly's exterior and manner were in every way military, even though he'd become an esteemed political figure. Although attractive, she had to assume that Asterly looked nothing like his renowned twin, Sir Harry. To be fair, Asterly's face had been permanently etched with the stress of his years at war but softened to become almost unrecognizable whenever he looked at his wife. Their connection to each other was as tangible as it was not appreciated in London society. The pair's transparent devotion produced a strange yearning in Beatrice's soul. She hoped that what she felt wasn't envy.

The men led the way as they crossed a vast, black-and-white checkered marble vestibule and climbed the staircase to an upper floor withdrawing room. Beatrice strained to overhear the men's conversation, the tone surprisingly jocular for two such formidable men.

"Tell me, Joss, was it love at first sight, like me and Lizzie?"

Beatrice heard the smile in Joss's voice when he eventually replied, "Do you know, Peregrine, I believe it was."

Heat filled her cheeks. She might have kicked him on the ankle for that. Joss knew she was listening to every word of the conversation and was picturing her stuck between the fence boards with her sit-upon wriggling to get free.

Lady Asterly took the lead when they reached the landing and conspiratorially murmured, "Lady Warfield, do you ever feel seized by the urge to deal your spouse a sharp rap on the knuckles?"

"Frequently, ma'am. You know the particulars then, the inherent joke?"

"Joss told us how you met. The piglet rescue. You have my permission to brain Joss with the closest object to hand, as long as you agree to call me Elizabeth and allow me to call you Beatrice. I believe I like that name as much as Joss. He talks incessantly about you."

Beatrice sent a meaningful glance over her shoulder at Joss. "Does he? You quite surprise me. Will there be many joining us this afternoon? I know it isn't your at home day."

"Only a few friends. Has Joss taken you around to the sites yet?"

"We have upcoming lectures at the Royal Institute. Otherwise he's been catching up with correspondence and such. And prying me from his library for meals."

Footmen swept open a set of double doors to a drawing room appointed in jade and gold silk and brocade. Porcelain urns overflowing with white roses and lilacs scented the air. The décor somehow managed to appear luxurious and yet understated. The subtlety captivated and gave indication for Joss's fascination with Elizabeth.

Lady Asterly asked as they crossed to a pair of couches, "You are a great reader?"

"It is the sole vocation left to me now that I am no longer obligated to Father's parish."

Beatrice sat where Lady Asterly indicated, while a tea tray was placed before them on a low table. The men escaped to a sideboard where they chose wine over tea.

"How do you take your tea, Beatrice?"

"I spy lemon. That would be lovely, thank you. Are you a reader, Elizabeth?"

"I rarely have the time."

"That is a pity." Beatrice tasted the tea, a wonderfully aromatic blend she'd never tasted before and assumed it came with a very dear price.

Lady Asterly held her teacup in the palm of hand, quite unusual, something one might see in the country but not in an etiquette-bound London setting. Beatrice liked her informal manner, found it relaxing in a strangely intimate way, as if she were now an insider in the Asterly faction.

"Why do you attribute it as a pity, Beatrice?"

"Selfishness on my part. It's ever a problem to find individuals with whom to converse about the classics, history, philosophy. Men won't have it, you know. This perverse obsession to study renders me something of a social trial."

"It may surprise you to learn that I fully understand your dilemma, since I have a dedicated and quite unfeminine interest in mathematics."

"Ah, a Pythagorean."

"Nothing so complex. More along the line of mind-numbing mediocrity." She continued with a hint of a grin and drollery, "I should think a mere bookkeeper better describes my penchant more accurately."

"Forgive me, Elizabeth, for contradicting, but I think not. My husband has a certain inflection, a warmth in his voice when he speaks of you. His admiration is most sincere, and he is not a man to give that lightly."

"If I heard that much admiration in my own

95

husband's manner of speaking about another lady, I wouldn't respond with your complacency. I take it that you are not easily provoked to jealousy."

"Not at all. I doubt Sir Jocelyn realizes that he categorizes people in how he addresses them. When speaking to my dear friend, Emily, he is quite gentle. She is sweet-natured and easily distressed. With you, he's frank in his admiration but with a *soupcon* of indulgent humor. When he greeted Lord Asterly this evening, great respect and conviviality. I believe he likes your husband very much."

"They have enjoyed a friendship for some years and share many political views. And may I be so impertinent to ask about Joss's manner when speaking to you?"

Beatrice paused to evaluate. "Circumspect at best. Logical, always, but if I take it in the way you meant, the man hasn't a romantic notion to call his own." Elizabeth's astonished then merry reaction caused Beatrice to hesitate again. "Did I say something amusing?"

"Not at all. It's only that your reply doesn't concur with...never mind. And forgive me, but your forthrightness is somewhat startling, even though Joss told us that you are invariably honest."

"It is good of him to say so. One shouldn't wish to be otherwise."

Elizabeth primly replied with a sparkle in her eyes, "Quite."

Beatrice titled her head to one side. "Did I say something else amusing?"

"Ah, no, but perhaps you may not have noticed that our spouses have sneaked up behind us to
96

eavesdrop."

Unconcerned, Beatrice selected a currant-loaded scone from the plate Elizabeth offered and gave a succinct response. "How like men with a political bent. Too invested in what others are saying. One must suspect that they do so to learn something to entrench and bolster their own positions. Have you invited more of your friends? I've read so much about them."

"Who in particular?"

"Earl Ravenswold and his wife. Lady Collyns and Sir Harry. Of course. I should like to ascertain for myself if he is the most handsome creature in England."

"I wouldn't go that far," Lord Asterly muttered behind them.

"Of course, he is," his wife countered. "And show some loyalty for your brother. Lady Ravenswold runs a close second to our Harry in beauty, but he isn't in town. Olivia, Lady Collyns, is. You will also meet Viscount Grieves and his wife today. Sir Cameron and Lady Bradford are in town. You will like Allison and must make a friend of her. She used to practice midwifery and now only does so for her friends."

The names began to blur together until she was later introduced to them and she could put faces and personalities to the names and titles. The men strolled off to somewhere they could smoke, drink, and talk about gentlemen's topics. Initially, Beatrice yearned to join them. Then she discovered that their wives were active women with decided opinions, involved in unusual but vital charities, and gifted with talents other than those she designated as mundane even though considered socially desirable.

She had much to think about on the drive back to Willows. Joss broke into her thoughts when he asked, "Give me your impressions of today, Bea."

"One must be impressed by the diversity alone. There is that tedious axiom about the eccentrics one invariably encounters in the country. The wives of your friends are in their own ways quite outside of what is considered the norm, which for me, is a tremendous relief. There is Lady Grieves, so blond and delicate, and yet she likes to shoot pistols. Extraordinary. And her history. She was at the same time a duchess in hiding and acting as dresser for Elizabeth. She graciously offered to assist with clothes. With her, perhaps that won't be as tiresome as I dreaded."

"What about Lizzie?"

"Elizabeth? She is fascinating and charming, but there is an undercurrent…a vague sense that one should never take her lightly. If one were in a dire fix, an insurmountable predicament of some sort, she could be relied upon for relief. Is that not right?"

"Precisely. And what of Olivia? I don't know Lady Bradford well and would like to hear about her also."

"Allison, Lady Bradford, a most intriguing female. It's as if she carries a sign stating that she is steadfast and yet rather fragile inside. There is something peculiar about her touch. Did you shake her hand? No? Well, if you had you would have felt that physical contact with her relays a sense of healing and comfort. An almost spiritual sensation and visceral at the same time. As Elizabeth advised, Allison's skill as a midwife will be most welcome when—"

In an attempt to overlook her abrupt cut off to avoid the subject of children, he quickly said, "You

98

haven't said anything about Lady Collyns. I thought the two of you were the most suited for friendship, her being a bishop's daughter."

Recovering poise, she replied, "Olivia, yes, we do share practical outlooks, but I think I will establish friendships with all of your friends' wives. Having spent my entire life around people who are very much alike, I most especially enjoyed the diversity. They are so confident and have such substantial traits. Lofty ambitions and goals. Olivia is a fervent abolitionist, and so is Sir Harry. Quite a surprise, and in another way, a disappointment."

When she quieted, he teased, "A disappointment, the grand Sir Harry? You cannot get away without explaining that cryptic remark."

"The disappointment lies in not having the opportunity to verify the endless prattle about his beauty. His appearance is so talked about that it has taken on a persona of its own. In contrast, Olivia is so practical and wise. The man can't be as superficial as he's made out to be, or she would never have married him."

Joss sourly admitted, "He isn't. It's a lie he concocted for reasons beyond my understanding. But his extraordinary looks cannot be denied."

"I should like to see a godlike man in person. Will he attend the party next week, do you think?"

"I have no idea, and I believe we've exhausted the subject of Harry. You see me relieved that you've made friends who will help you acclimate to city life, but don't expect too much in the way of conversation at next week's assembly. And before I forget, Elizabeth dealt me a sound scolding for not taking you around to

99

the sites."

She held up her hand. "Please, sir, no Astley's Amphitheatre nor the Tower, and definitely not Hedleys Puffing Billy. Kensington Gardens, perhaps. I much prefer the upcoming lecture topics Evans procured from the Royal Institute. Unfortunately, I cannot attend unaccompanied and not confident the ladies I met today would be interested in the reduction of materials to isolate a basic element."

"Most likely not, but I would. Consider yourself accompanied."

Chapter 12

The Saturday evening of the party at Asterly House arrived faster than Beatrice wanted. She had assumed before leaving home that her days as a wife would settle into a life of tedious repetition, the dreaded mundane. Instead, every day at Willows came filled with correspondence to answer, a house to make her own and one much larger than what she was accustomed, which took more time to manage.

She'd become resigned to the need to shop for clothes. Happily, Evangeline had agreed to accompany her. Lord Grieves, her mostly silent husband, Armwinger Freddie, a famous duelist, surprisingly acted as their escort.

Beatrice didn't know how to categorize the viscount. Hatless, his long, fine hair floated around his head like a black cloud. Brilliant sapphire eyes lazily surveyed the world with derisive weariness. He spoke only when addressed, silently bored but latently lethal. His viscountess, petite, whip-smart, and quite Gallic in her mannerisms and way of speaking, was the only thing that interested him. When they stood together, they made an eye-catching couple, he so dashing and dangerous and she fair and elegant.

Beatrice couldn't imagine presenting any sort of impression when she stood beside Joss. She would always be an ordinary country girl. It was difficult to believe what Elizabeth insisted—that in time, after penetrating the ranks of the ton—she would be set down as an Original. Original what, Beatrice couldn't begin to suppose. She certainly didn't feel original.

Evangeline had done her best, selecting colors and fabrics, suggesting styles a la mode, but in the end, Beatrice only wanted to go home to Willows, settle in with a book, or perhaps have an ice at Gunter's before leaving the city.

Arriving late due to traffic, she and Joss entered Asterly House, where Joss waved off a maid and removed her cloak himself. They were told there was no reception line and that Lady Asterly expected them.

"Beatrice, you must always wear that shade of blue," Joss whispered as he handed off her cape. "What it does for your eyes is beyond description."

She placed her gloved hand on his arm as they crossed the foyer's black-and-white checked marble. Anxiety about how she would appear to his cadre of intriguing friends began to gnaw at her nerves. She didn't care for her own sake, but in the short time she'd been married to Joss, she came to realize that she owed him a great deal and obliged to be the sort of wife who must bring embarrassment to his name.

"Thank you, but credit must be given to Lady Grieves. She had a marvelous time riffling through pattern books and choosing fabrics. She did the work. I merely stood there like an insentient mannequin, while getting punctured with a thousand pins."

"Truly, a thousand? Did you count them?"

She ignored that. "Carter was in transports opening the boxes and parcels. I thought she might faint from joy."

"Then you have become the perfect employer. A credit to your servant. And you are, Beatrice, quite lovely tonight."

She had to gently clear her throat in order to say, "Thank you."

"Are you nervous?"

That goaded any lack of assurance. "Whatever for?"

He silently laughed as they reached the top of the staircase. He nodded his head in a bow as Elizabeth swept through the drawing room doors to greet them.

"Ah, the couple of the evening."

Beatrice's spirits lifted when Elizabeth leaned forward to touch cheeks in greeting. "We apologize for the tardiness. Traffic congestion is a new experience for me. Have we ruined your evening?"

"Certainly not. Joss, Asterly has something to ask you then come find me. And Beatrice, I would suggest a gradual immersion into the assembled. I shall introduce you to Lady Criswell first. She may sound distrait at times, but she is a kind soul and a marvelous harpist. She will play for us later this evening."

"I look forward to hearing it. I have no musical talents whatsoever but admire them greatly in others. I fear my lack of artistic talents may be a source of hardship when it comes to acting as a ton hostess."

Elizabeth looped her arm through Beatrice's as they strolled into the room, a subtle statement and silent announcement that she was a particular friend, not merely a guest. The ingenious and thoughtful gesture warmed and bolstered her faltering spirits as well as inspiring admiration for Joss's clever friend—now, by association, hers also—an astonishing epiphany.

"You must not allow trivialities to become worrisome, Beatrice. Keep in mind that almost every weakness can be turned into an advantage. I will introduce you to the most talented of my friends and acquaintances. Then a successful gathering becomes as easy as sending an invitation. Artists love to perform. Encourage them to entertain, and there you are. Everyone will think you a clever and generous hostess. Ah, here is Lady Criswell. I suspect the two of you have interests in common. Her late aunt hails from your father's parish."

Lady Criswell was blessed with a vast amount of silver-shot chestnut hair piled high on her head, the arrangement pierced with purple and green ostrich plumes. Matronly and kind-faced, her plump figure filled out a jade and mauve evening gown embellished with many flounces around the hem.

Beatrice suppressed a comment about how that good lady had chosen the colors for her gown so as not to clash with the décor. As they exchanged comments regarding the appointments of the room, the number of guests, the usual acceptable topics, Beatrice quickly warmed to Lady Criswell's kindly disposition and liked her even more when she discovered an ally in the preference for country living. She felt herself quite at home with a new friend when Elizabeth had to excuse herself to greet more guests.

When Joss and Lord Asterly gravitated toward a trio of gentlemen on the other side of the drawing room entrance, Beatrice turned slightly on the couch seat to give her companion her full attention.

Lady Criswell fluttered and beamed when Beatrice asked, "What will you be playing for us this evening? I am so looking forward to hearing it. Lady Asterly was singing your praises as we came into the room."

They enjoyed a comfortable exchange about their respective districts until interrupted. Beatrice stood to greet them, squashing disappointment when she recognized Lady Richardson. Anticipation glinted in the woman's eyes as she introduced the lady with her. "If you will pardon the intrusion, Lady Criswell, I should like to present my friend to your companion. Lady Alis has expressed a decided interest in meeting someone so gifted with culinary skills."

Lean, elegant, but unfortunately unhandsome, Lady Alis displayed her perfect teeth in a not quite smile, something more like a toothy snarl. "It is a pleasure to finally meet the hostess who so impressed her company with a dessert made with her very own hands. How quaint. Is this a new custom in the countryside, Miss Allardyce?"

Nervous from the apparent tension, Lady Criswell gently corrected, "Forgive me, Lady Alis, but she's recently married to Sir Jocelyn Warfield."

~~~

On the other side of the room, Elizabeth murmured, "Poor Beatrice. I should have invited scholars to keep your wife occupied."

"She's not a four-year-old, Lizzie."

"Joss, please, truly look at what is transpiring over there. Something is quite wrong. Beatrice's eyes have glazed over, either from boredom or she is distancing herself. It is unfortunate others intruded. She was doing perfectly well with Lady Criswell, who has no conversation but is so very sweet-natured."

"Who is the female who considers her consequence higher than everyone else's in the room?"

"Oh, yes. That is Lady Alis. She was reared in

ducal splendor and considers herself above most people with the exception of royalty. Dowling married her for the dowry, not the consequence. He's of the opinion that he has enough of his own, but needed the funds to support political aims. She has an uninvited friend in tow. I believe it's Richardson's wife."

"You are friends with Lady Richardson?"

"Not at all. Nor Lady Alis. Peregrine said Dowling and Richardson inveigled invitations for this evening. Actually were quite insistent. Something to do with Richardson's upcoming bill regarding the canal system. I'm not well acquainted with any of them, but Lady Alis has attended a few parties here. She's not astute and often parrots opinions that she supposes make her appear witty. Peregrine does the return calls in my stead, since the connection is more with the husbands than I with their wives. Oh, dear. One can tell from here that something is not quite what it should be."

No longer employing her best feature in a parody of a smile, Lady Alis's nasal, carrying voice sliced through the conversational hum. "What an unusual pairing, Lady Warfield, you and Sir Jocelyn. One should think he would acquire a spouse more experienced in what is necessary in an exemplary society hostess. But then, what passes in the country for refinement cannot be expected nor compared to what is considered *de rigueur* in town."

The room quieted as Beatrice paused to answer. Joss scanned the room for reactions. The Asterly evenings were known for their political brilliance, artistic discussions and presentations. Sniping—other than what arose during a heated debate—wasn't a common occurrence. Stunned anticipation intensified the silence.

In her typically blunt way, Beatrice finally said, "I am curious, Lady Alis. Do you typically have success with a derogatory form of interrogation in lieu of good manners?"

Lady Alis stared, startled. "I beg your pardon?"

"As you should. That insult was not at all veiled. In any case, I am never moved by bullying tactics, but I confess to an interest as to how this approach works for you in social settings. A personalized, empirical appraisal, if you will."

Lady Alis now gaped. Beatrice mowed over the poor woman's attempt to reply. "One should think that the mere skirting of the object of an insult is a coward's ploy, but then, so is any attempt to humiliate another person. It's also a rather inefficient way to express one's disdain. There is nothing quite like honesty. If you have an opinion, ma'am, speak your mind. Clarity is all."

On the other side of the room, Elizabeth turned her head to the side to quell a choked laugh. When she briefly squeezed Joss's wrist, he knew the move wasn't noticed. Every eye in the room stayed riveted on the byplay that included Lady Criswell's mortified surprise to be caught in the crossfire then followed with her rapid escape to her husband's side. The spiteful gleam in Lady Richardson's eyes was enough to send anyone with sense out of the range of verbal shrapnel. Lady Alis stood in frozen disbelief, sporting a fixed, saccharine grin, her mind an obvious blank.

Elizabeth whispered, "Oh, Joss, perhaps you should intervene."

Joss felt a smile curving his mouth. Beatrice's

scarcely concealed boredom had vanished, replaced with acute curiosity. She wore her *let's-discuss-that-assumption* level-eyed expression.

He removed the monocle to better view what was about to happen. "Observe, Lizzie."

Lady Richardson was speaking but in a much lower voice, her malicious intent apparent from across the room. Lady Alis continued to look bewildered as to how to retake lost ground but found no headway as Beatrice focused on Lady Richardson's smarmy grin. Lady Alis's attempts to interject were finally heard but quickly ignored when the previous contention between Beatrice and Lady Richardson resumed. When Lady Alis again tried to insert a word, Beatrice quietly replied with something that made that woman blanch and gasp.

As the tableau of an uncomfortably stilted conversation continued, Elizabeth whispered, "Oh, Joss, rescue that poor woman."

"My Bea can take care of herself."

"I didn't mean her. Bring your intended to heel before she mutilates Lady Alis beyond repair. The woman's nothing to me, but Peregrine might need her husband for a quid pro quo in future."

He couldn't help inserting a wry reprimand in his reply. "Then you might consider doing a better job of masking your enjoyment of the spectacle and see to it for yourself."

"I can't! I'll collapse into laughter if I go over there."

"And I remind you that Lady Alis is your guest, Lizzie."

"And her ladyship's tormentor is *your* wife."
108

"Very well, I shall perform the honors, but it's a joy to watch Beatrice discharge her cannons with her typical artlessness. Excuse me. I'm off to do your duty."

As he stepped away, he peripherally noticed his hostess applying a handkerchief as if muffling a cough, when he knew she dabbed at tears of laughter. The rest of the room was just coming back to life from petrified astonishment. He wished that he could have better heard his valiant wife shearing down the heartless bit of snobbery that was Lady Alis and Lord Richardson's viper-tongued wife. Lizzie's guests had watched in rapt amazement of the display of a social scion's set down, if not a verbal cut direct, something rarely seen at an Asterly gathering. Bea had no idea that she'd created a scene of epic proportions.

Surprised concern slowed his pace when Beatrice's expression suddenly became stricken. She abruptly pulled her gaze from Lady Richardson's to his approach then flicked a glance at Elizabeth. In the next instant, she wiped away all emotional response but only after giving him an oddly appraising look. His arrival ended something Lady Richardson was whispering, no doubt spiteful.

He bowed slightly to the ladies. "If you will pardon me, Lady Alis, Lady Richardson, I should like to show my wife a sculpture newly arrived from Greece. She's vastly interested in all things Greek."

Beatrice instantly riveted her attention onto anything that would allow her to escape the tedium of two idiots. Thankfully, she didn't say as much out loud, but her expression screamed exasperation.

Desperate to reinstate her dignity, Lady Alis

inserted, "Lady Asterly has acquired an Elgin?"

Before Beatrice could make a pointed correction about the Elgin statuary being in the possession of Elgin and no one else, he said, "It is my understanding Lady Asterly purchased the item directly from the proper authorities in Greece. Please excuse us."

Conversation in the room resumed when Joss captured Beatrice's elbow and gently but firmly guided her away from another social calamity.

As they stepped out into the passageway, Beatrice muttered, "Lady Richardson is the devil's spawn. I think she used that silly person in a cowardly attempt to cause me discomfort. I shall have to seek her out and see to her officiousness."

"No, Bea, but she will be hearing from me. She used Lady Criswell dreadfully and you weren't much nicer."

"I? I was merely hoping to ascertain if my inquisitor meant to subject a person to cruelty in the form of a societal methodology. In retrospect, I doubt she has the wits to affect a specific stratagem for bullying. And I will have you understand that I rise to every instance of maltreatment, sir. Maimonides made his opinions on persecution quite clear."

"Beatrice, you were pulling the wings from a fly."

"That is a sickening...wait!" She'd dug in her heels, forcing him to halt. "Am I guilty of the same behavior?"

He looked down into her genuine concern. "I don't think you did so with humiliation aforethought. It was apparent to me and to Lizzie that you were intolerably encumbered with their company and leaping upon the first interesting idea."

110

"I might not have been so excessively bored had the tiresome Lady Alis not insisted on bragging about her husband, who has not proved himself to be as intelligent as his much vaunted reputation. After scanning through his bill, I read some of his other writings, which in many ways are sadly undeveloped and poorly attributed. A number of his conclusions cannot be considered well reasoned."

With an encouraging tug, he again got her moving away from the scene of the massacre. "Where did you come across his bill?"

"Sitting on your desk. But if it is as you say, and I did do Lady Alis a disservice, I must apologize. Papa would expect no less and demand that I transcribe at least thirty Scriptural instances of penitence."

She was still talking when he led her across the gallery to the viewing area where Elizabeth's private statuary and art works were displayed. Finding the room well-lit for the evening, he closed the door.

Bea immediately moved deeper into the room, her head swiveling, gaping and gawking at Lizzie's personal collection of paintings and sculpture. A white marble statue partially swathed in dark green material stopped her. She stared up, her curiosity caught. As if in a daze, she yanked on the slick material, which slithered to pool on the floor. She inhaled a startled gasp at the nearly nude male. An unfurled scroll covered the unmentionables in the front but not the bare backside, which her irrepressible curiosity demanded that she evaluate.

Emotion exploded vibrant energy low in his belly, spreading upward to send rippling power throughout his chest and down his arms. He didn't recognize jealousy for what it was at first, the strong animalistic push to immediately react. Her continued entrallment with a naked man wasn't helping him subdue the sudden response.

"What a magnificent piece but I think not ancient. It must be recently done, but his figure is very Greek in execution. What a remarkable work. One must wonder at his expression, so sad and contemplative. Do you know the artist?"

She paid no attention to his tone when he tightly answered, "No, but the subject is Harry Collyns."

"Oh, my word. Then it is indeed true. He is astonishingly beautiful and his physique exactly like the youthful athletes of glorious Grecian times."

"How does a country miss become so knowledgeable of the male form?"

"Illustrations in books. Greek classics often have them, but Sir Harry's limbs and musculature are so uniform and pleasantly formed." She glided her palm down Harry's calf. "Much nicer than the illustrations. Now I am doubly sorry not to have met him tonight."

Joss dryly murmured, "Especially since he would have been clothed."

Her fascination transfixed, she missed the sarcasm. "Indeed, and how extraordinary for Olivia. I wonder if she finds it commonplace after a time, having this in front of her face all day, every day. I doubt I should."

There was no other way he could think of to get her to stop talking about Harry so he kissed her.

Chapter 13

Other than her father, she'd never been kissed by a man. Joss had given her a barely there touch on her cheek after the wedding ceremony. Nothing in the way of intimacy had occurred since then, other than the time spent inside a closed carriage, and that had been physically unsettling. Decidedly so, but also enlightening. Previously, close proximity to a man had never aroused a physical response.

This abrupt method of ending a conversation with a kiss had been startling, the sudden sealing of his mouth over hers. The firm pressure was followed by a lightness in the application of his lips, tender movements that gradually intensified until his arms came about her, bringing her firmly against his chest. Curiosity's constant quest for understanding melted into absorption of what a proper kiss involved. Attention to studying the details blurred with the awareness of how her body conformed to his. Without thought or instruction, she'd become pliable, acquiescing to the pressure of his tightening embrace. Her hands somehow knew what her inexperience did not, sliding up and around his shoulders to discover the texture of the hair fringing his jacket collar. Unexpected heat washed through her when she felt a fine quiver shivering the length of his body. After her light, investigative caress, Joss became man at his most elemental, excited by her, an ordinary country girl with no finesse or understanding of what was entailed on an intimate level.

He retreated enough to whisper, "Open your mouth, Bea. Let me show you how this is done."

When she did as he asked, she was grateful he held her so firmly. Her legs turned to water. She discovered herself hanging in his embrace, giving him right of entry to persuasively teach, until the moment was ruined, demolished with the intrusive memory of Lady Richardson's recent, poisonous words.

You are aware of his reputation. So keenly sought after with the ladies. As handy with them as with the reins, it's said.

The memory, its viciousness, chilled then scalded. Her husband had been with other women, kissed them, gained expertise and gratification from so many before her. The knowledge drenched her in humiliation. His reputation and the distasteful, and somehow shaming, information obliterated the tenderness of the moment, the excitement of newfound delight.

Even more disturbing, Lady Alis had as much as called her a bumpkin, which hadn't bothered at the time, but what if Joss made comparisons? She had no female wiles, no understanding of what a man considered alluring, other than easy availability. There was nothing about her person to attract him. He'd never made any overtures when it came to the physical aspects of marriage, other than the chaste kiss on the cheek at the conclusion of the wedding ceremony. It was quite obvious that he'd kissed her now to get her to stop jabbering about the statue.

She inwardly cringed at the awkwardness of the moment and her ignorance. His knowledge of women was revealed when he retreated, stepping back the instant he sensed her withdrawal.

"That quieted my busy Bea."

Her cheeks tingled then burned from the insinuation that she was a child that needed correction. "I am not your anything, sir."

"Of course you are, Beatrice. You're my wife."

She swallowed to force down the urge to weep. "And you no doubt would have been happier with a more amenable spouse."

His tender expression became remote. "If I desired treacle, I would have married it. A constant diet of sweetness palls over time. I've always preferred the tart."

"If the term applies to your prior female connections—"

"You allude to past liaisons? They were all ladies of high standing in society, even if they had the character, experience and constitutions of harlots. As I said, I would rather have the savory rather than the sweet." He ran a swift gaze over her figure. "Although I've no doubt you'll taste as sweet as necessary in all the right places. Ah, I have shocked you. Your cheeks have gone quite rosy."

She pinched her lips to hold in the retort. He smirked and took a step closer, softly teasing, "Go on, Miss Bea. Slap me. You know you want to."

Flustered, she blurted, "I detest promiscuous, vulgar behavior. There, are you satisfied?"

"Not nearly."

His low reply sounded like a purring growl,

sparking an irrational thrill. Even though he showed no outward sign, she sensed he was aware of the distress rampant inside her chest, and that provoked her into speaking impulsively.

"You are no gentleman. A man of integrity would never take pleasure in oversetting a lady and you do so at every turn. You stand there, cold and unreachable, utterly pleased with your taunts and provocations. A bully and a coward, that's what you are."

He took a step closer. "And what would you have me be? A languishing, soft-hearted lover? Perhaps you'd prefer a composer of vapid poetry? A theme dedicated to your nose or the pretty curve of your left ear. Although, it does have a pink softness that tempts. No, my preferences lie elsewhere on the female anatomy. Shall I list them?"

Her response was prefaced by a thin shriek of protest, which was as embarrassing as it was riling. The images his suggestions stirred up kept her frozen in place, unable to spout a roiling flood of outrage.

His soft laugh cooled the heat of her emotions. "Run, little girl, but it will do you no good. You should have been warned that I get what I want when I want it."

She backed up, whirled to escape, less afraid of him than the urge to run to him and discover what he meant, but he caught her arm.

"There is a fire inside you, Beatrice, and I've made myself the lucky man to stoke it."

"That kind of crude remark is exactly the sort of masculine supposition one would expect from a man like you."

"A man like me? What sort is that? I ask, not out

116

of curiosity, but with the secure knowledge that you will tell me precisely what you think."

How she disliked that smirk. Something about it, so smug and superior, sparked an internal quivering, a simmering that focused her temper. "Very well then, sir. I will speak my mind. You are the worst sort of male, boastful, arrogant, and preening."

He interrupted her by placing a finger across her mouth. Smiling, he murmured, "It cannot be boasting when it's the truth."

She batted his hand aside. "It is intolerable, disgraceful that you take pride in being a philanderer."

"Ah, the critical spirit fully emerges, but I disagree. You see before you the very model of a dutiful husband. No mistress. No paramours. Only a reluctant wife."

Paramours. The way he said it brought back Lady Richardson's glee, the triumphant sneer that prefaced the false concern in her parting shot.

Clever girl. You've caught the distinguished Sir Jocelyn. One hopes you understand how marriages are handled and do not have your head filled with childish dreams of love attained. He is keenly sought after, you know, with all the ladies. As handy with them as with the reins, it's said. One wonders how Lord Asterly tolerates Sir Jocelyn running tame under his own roof.

Even though she'd concealed the painful shock of that barb, the ugliness of its implications continued to simmer in wait for an outlet. Growing suspicion about Joss and Elizabeth aggravated the hurt, the scare of having married a man without principle, the pain of being taken in by her new friend, Elizabeth.

What if Joss's exterior hid something unpleasant

underneath? What did that say about her? She feared she was drawn to him anyway, whether a man of honor or not. And it hurt to be called reluctant when she was mainly anxious about the possibility of comparison and her ignorance. Books never explained it adequately, and Emily's description of what went on in the marriage bed made her feel even more inadequate and ill-prepared.

He smiled, his hazel eyes darkening, as he surveyed her from the floor up. "What? There is something about your expression. Are you reconsidering? Are you ruing a hasty decision to marry an unknown, a subject you couldn't pin down with an empirical study?"

"Do not mock me, sir. You have no moral high ground here. You cannot deny that you wasted your youth and good name with sporting diversions when you had obligations to your title, of which you gave no respect by flaunting your reputation."

When he leaned in she refused to budge, to retreat. She'd never been afraid of bullies, but this kind of persuasive intimidation was unlike any she'd ever encountered. Directly in front of her nose was pristine linen tied in an intricate knot, a wide span of shoulders, a hint of cologne, and a reminder. She'd briefly seen another side of him in the chaise when he showed her the pistol. At that moment, and now, she saw him as someone who could be unpredictable when thwarted.

His breath stirred her hair when he asked in a voice dark and coaxing, "So, tell me what you've heard, Lady Warfield."

When she pinched her lips shut in refusal, his husky laugh brushed over her face. "Got you there,
118

don't I, my prickly Bea. Unwilling to utter such unspeakable things? Don't let old tattle bother you. Gossip regarding me is ancient by London standards. I wager it was that viperous Lady Richardson spreading her venom. Let me think back. Is it the one when I broke all records and the hearts of my best team on a race from Brighton to London? Or the one where I floored Jackson with a punishing left? How about the one where I went through three wives at a Quorum hunting party and left them so satisfied that they were too exhausted to ask for more?"

Horrified, not by the listing of disgraceful behavior, but more by images she couldn't suppress, she gaped. When he leaned down to murmur against her shock-parted lips, her fluttering heart began to pound an erratic beat against her ribs.

"Here is my confession, my prickly and delectable Bea. The one about Gentleman Jackson is an exaggeration. Secondly, I would never push my horses to the point of damaging their lungs or breaking their spirit. And the last one," he paused to softly laugh in a way that made the fine hairs on the back of her neck rise, "that last one I will admit against every rule of gentlemanly discretion…is absolutely true."

She swallowed and forced a steadiness in her reply that she in no way felt. "Is that some sort of warning?"

"More on the order of…let us say…advice?"

When he straightened to his full height, unreasonable disappointment took hold of her temper. Even though she was mainly annoyed with herself for feeling disappointed, she directed her frustration at the nearest target.

"You…you are a disgrace, sir! Of absolutely no

credit to your gender, a bounder and a blackguard. I put it to you that no female of decency would have anything to do with your person or with your lack of honorable conduct."

Something flickered in his eyes, a flash that erased the smolder, changing it to ice. She felt her own eyes widen when he said through his teeth, "Beware of insulting me, Beatrice. I take pleasure succeeding with any kind of challenge."

"What I said was a statement, not a challenge."

"And I take no insult from hypocrites."

She jerked free. "Hypocrite? I am not and furthermore have no intention of adding my name to your list of conquests!"

"The reply to that is a foregone conclusion. We're married."

"Am I to feel complimented, sir, to be placed as a peer with the rest of your paramours?"

A premonition, a hot and instinctive alertness sizzled down her spine when he whispered, "And I know women, wife. You're no saint or prude. It's latent, but I vow that you will let me prove you are and savor the taking when I do."

She collected her dignity. Since he was too tall to look down her nose, she hiked up her chin and larded her reply with scorn. "Typical male conceit. You do not surprise, sir."

When she made to leave, he whirled her around. A puff of air burst free with a startled squeak when he tugged her forward against the solid wall of his chest. His mouth slanted over hers. She'd expected this kiss to hurt, but the pressure was softly insistent, coaxing, gentle, while his hold felt like a tender vise.

Robbed of will, her surprise-widened eyes drooped shut. She dissolved into an experience unlike the previous embrace. Where that kiss had been sweet and searching, this scorched and blinded. The tip of his tongue skimmed sensitive tissues inside her lips. When her lips parted, he entered her mouth. She inhaled a gasp and his arms tightened to hold her still. This kiss persuaded, enticing her to give in, to participate. From far away she heard a muffled moan. The fact that such a sound came from her was obliterated by what a kiss from a too-knowledgeable man could do to an untutored recipient. The analytical part of her mind sought to dissect what was occurring, but pleasure dissolved all thoughts. Her body relaxed, responding to his with a will other than her own. She sank into the experience, letting him guide her arms up and around his neck. One hand spanned her upper back, pressing her bosom into his chest, the other lower, pinning her in place. She could feel him, all of him, from knees to shoulders. He encased her in a cage of steel-armed strength. Helpless, she allowed his mouth to feast on hers, creating responses, sensations that obliterated resistance and erased all rational thought.

When he suddenly let her go, she stood swaying in place, blinking up at a stranger. His suave confidence had disappeared, replaced by a fierce determination that poured thrilling understanding throughout her system. She'd been a fool, a complete idiot to cross swords and intellect with this man. She'd married a chameleon, a man who by class and culture was endowed and imbued with privileges she would never have, could never aspire to achieve. He was a firmly entrenched member of the ton, and she, the naive offspring of a country parson. Where she was intelligent, he was wily and practiced, accustomed to having his way in all things, capable of ruthlessness to achieve any objective of his liking. Somehow, during the first days of their acquaintance, she'd become one.

Seeing her stunned condition, he slowly smiled, like a predator lazily studying his prey, and slowly drew her back into his arms.

"Now you understand, don't you, my prickly Bea. You can't hide anything from me. Let's celebrate our first marital spat. For your insatiable edification, this is what is known as kiss and make-up."

Her pride and temper sprang to life. She shoved out of his hold, despising that she could do so only because he allowed it. "You still haven't bested me!"

She hated that she'd sounded weepy, because the truth was that she felt on the verge of tears. And afraid. And physically, horribly deprived of something she couldn't name or fully comprehend due to her irritating ignorance.

He shook his head and silently laughed. "Poor darling, you'll bend to me because I can give you everything you've ever dreamed of having, so many impossible yearnings while shut away in your safe, little closet in the country."

Determined not to give in to a bout of tears, she searched for a scathing retort. "That is nothing less than what a man of your ilk would say. Just another male braying how it is entirely the woman's fault for tempting him."

"No, Beatrice. I'm sure you have many imaginings that you consider shocking, but I would find your girlish daydreams beyond tepid. I was speaking about

122

something else. Your secret yearnings to become a respected author. Ah, you're amazed that I haven't forgotten our pact?"

When she pinched her lips shut, refusing to speak, he visibly relaxed and smiled. "You'll be even more amazed and intrigued to know that I didn't lie. I do have a company ready to publish your essays. What? Still nothing to say?"

With ill-grace and through gritted teeth, she muttered, "Thank you."

He inhaled a deep breath and slowly exhaled. Like the chameleon she suspected he could be, his features altered when he looked up from his thoughtful study of the floor. "Very well. I think we understand each other a bit more. Let us collect ourselves and return to the party."

"I would prefer to go home."

"Can't say as I blame you. It's been an eventful evening, and I haven't yet had the pleasure of destroying the unpleasant Lady Richardson."

"Yes. It's due to her interference that we have been placed in this regrettable situation." When she noticed the wince of his good eye, she said, "I apologize. That was indelicate. You must know what I mean. The woman does need to be constrained from the pleasure she takes in ruining others. She has no care for the damage she causes."

Taking her arm and reaching for the door latch, he ruefully added, "And what must be done to make the repairs to wherever she has laid waste. Chin up, my lady. It's time to trim that woman's wick, if Elizabeth hasn't already done so."

As they retraced their way back to the party, she

asked, "Why would she do that?"

"Because, Beatrice, you are now a friend of Lady Asterly, and anyone daring to hurt one of her own flirts with devastation. As you suspected after your introduction, she takes no prisoners."

When they returned to the guests, Lady Richardson and her husband were absent. Lady Alis kept company with those on a par with her social level and avoided speaking or looking at Bea. This was a relief, as was listening to Lady Criswell's talent with the harp strings. Following that, Joss was inveigled into singing, accompanied by Elizabeth, who was so accomplished that she could send flirting glances her husband's way.

Beatrice attempted to find tranquility in the fluid beauty of Joss's voice. She couldn't stop looking back, seeking to unravel what had transpired while standing under the marble gaze of the most beautiful masculine figure she'd ever seen. Something had set up Joss's back. Oddly, nothing about Sir Harry was as attractive or physically arresting as the rarified sight of her husband's gaze when it smoldered.

A strange thought came—could it be jealousy? But how could that be? And what of that insinuation of an illicit involvement with Lady Asterly?

Instead of only listening, she studied Joss. He didn't stand too closely to Lady Asterly as he sang, never came close to touching her when he reached to turn the pages of music. He did exchange a smile with her at one point but mostly paid attention to the lyrics. They finished to more than merely polite applause. He offered his hand when she rose from the tufted piano seat. They exchanged smiles, hers unabashedly affectionate, his brilliant.

124

He never smiled like that unless something brought him great pleasure. This would bear watching.

Chapter 14

No matter how he tried, Joss couldn't get his thoughts away from what happened in the private gallery. He talked and sang, but mentally, he was still in that room in front of that blasted statue. Every time he tried to erase the memory he was launched back to the incident. No amount of sluicing a cold wash of reason over an inferno of internal chaos helped. His reaction to Beatrice's appreciation of another man sparked a side of his personality he hadn't realized existed.

At first, he didn't recognize the grinding emotion that slipped free the leash he always kept on stronger feelings. He'd never suffered from jealousy before today. He was still striving to understand his compulsion to always be close to Beatrice, to know where she was, that she was within reach. There seemed to be no way to combat the worrisome pit of anxiety that writhed within whenever he didn't know where she was. He'd successfully hidden this bizarre and unexplainable need to stay connected to and with her at all times. The compulsion had crept up on him gradually, until becoming a pervasive part of his life, something beyond his control. He didn't like feeling helpless, unsure.

Beatrice had a natural knack for stoking latent

feelings better left unexpressed and deeply buried. He wasn't an idiot and made the connection with how his father had forced a separation from Joss and his mother. Beatrice had no inkling of how painful that kind of separation had been; she'd been wholly and unconditionally adored by her only parent.

He'd examined her as she'd stood at the private art room's closed door, chin up, waiting for him to open it, making the attempt to project cool poise. But he knew his Bea. Anxious and unsure, she struggled not to grind her teeth and fixed ruthless focus on the supposed superiority of her intellect. She had no idea that her appreciation of Harry and his bared ass had turned his vision red and viscera inside out.

Unfortunately for her, he could read her every emotion. He had no problem seeing how she felt. In that respect, she was clear as glass. She waved truth like a flag, but her specific thoughts about him, how she felt about him, were not easily discerned. Her contempt for his past behaviors, and a reputation so old it was almost forgotten, stung. It hadn't helped his cause that his vibrant and unexpected hurt caused a reaction that had been rash, but her disdain and remote superiority undid the containment of an old wound— his father's disregard and contempt of a son's affection for his mother.

His father considered a boy's attachment to his mother obscene and said so often. His opinion was that women were meant for three things—pleasure, providing heirs, and a substantial dowry. As a lad, Joss had listened with disgust. In contrast, he suffered from the constant and irritating need for his father's respect, a yearning that never waned, even when bombarded with the man's revolting tirades.

His father had been cold-hearted and utterly selfish. Joss had worked his entire life to eradicate those traits, and yet the empty hole remained. Bea's lack of respect had opened an ancient wound, and it made no sense. Even more than the yearning for his father's respect, he desired esteem from his Beatrice. When he finally had his mother to himself for the last years of her life, she poured over him all the love and affection she hadn't been allowed to give. He'd been perfect in her eyes.

He wasn't whimsical, and yet one of his wife's most attractive qualities was her pragmatic view on every idea that came her way. She didn't leap to any conclusion. She pondered what she'd heard from all sides and made a decision. Why he found that impossibly erotic escaped his understanding.

Perhaps he shouldn't have given his mistress her conge. If he hadn't paid her off, then he wouldn't be in this ridiculous state over his wife. He knew he was fooling himself. He could never break that vow while married to Bea, no matter that she thought he could and would. Or already had.

He was absolutely sure that his suggestion to postpone consummation was an idea spawned by idiocy. At the time, he'd been willing to offer up a limb for acceptance of his proposal. He'd wanted her from the first sight of her bottom wriggling to back out of the fence's clutch. The joke had been on him when Peregrine asked if it had been love at first sight. It wasn't that he had a particular attraction to any female's derriere. He liked everything about the female body. It was that Beatrice's mind was connected to the

128

object of what was becoming uncontrollable obsession, or more accurately, lust.

How extraordinary, a husband lusting after his wife. He'd witnessed the condition in his friends, Ravenswold's the most shocking. The earl, a placid giant, couldn't be provoked for any reason, unless it involved his wife. Considered the best shot in all of England, no one goaded Viscount Grieves into a duel. Sir Harry had come close to skewering a former suitor of his Puritanical Olivia. Everyone knew Asterly kept a stiletto hidden down the side of his boot, a habit unable to give over from his spying days, and there was an air about Peregrine. Anyone involved in espionage for over seven years had to have learned how to kill, quietly and efficiently.

So perhaps it wasn't all that ridiculous that he would find it provoking when the woman he desired made remarks—no, she droned on and on with glowing adjectives for another man—that he might go off his head a bit. Maybe more than a bit. It had been a near thing that he hadn't thrown her over a display case and presumed on his husbandly rites. What had cooled his ardor was the stunning discovery that she'd never been kissed on the mouth. She'd kept her lips firmly pressed in a line, at first, then she oozed into delicious relaxation. That exquisite melting into one's arms, the signal that cried out to any red-blooded male that it was time to press forward. It had been a near thing, if not for the warning inside his head that he held a woman who knew next to nothing about sex. For her, it should not be carnal; the act itself had to be respectful, gentle, about love-making. Heady, sweaty rutting, no matter how much he desired it, was not for his Bea.

Her voice jarred him out of his imagination. She stood so cool and remote, waiting at the gallery doorway. "I believe you said that we were leaving?"

How long had he been standing here, trying sort through the jumble inside his head?

"A moment, please."

He picked up the slick green material pooled on the floor beneath the statute and tossed it over Harry.

She raised an eyebrow. "There are other works in here far more revealing."

"They're dead. Harry isn't."

"That is correct. I am sure Elizabeth wouldn't want her brother by marriage ogled in the manner one would a typical artifact. Even though he's more beautiful than any of the others."

He clenched his teeth to suppress another searing flash of jealousy and twisted stiff lips into what might pass for a smile. She cast him an odd glance as they made their way back to the party, quickly dismissing whatever he'd not been able to conceal.

It was past time to get himself well in hand. Whereas he might alter a fact or basic truth to fit his needs, he tried very hard to never lie to himself. Her lack of esteem for him hurt worse than the memory of his father's lack of humanity. What he'd endured throughout boyhood made him vow to never be distant with his children. A thrill sliced through his vitals at the thought of making children with Bea.

Chapter 15

Beatrice paused on the flight of steps leading down to the Royal Institute's foyer when Joss asked, "Bea, where is your reticule?"

Lifting her arm, she saw that nothing dangled from her wrist. "Oh, I must have taken it off and left it in the lecture theatre. Now I recall. I set it down beside the seat after withdrawing my notebook."

"Would you rather go back with me or wait in the foyer while I fetch it?"

"In the foyer, please. There is an interesting display near the entrance I would like to see before we leave."

Taking her arm, he escorted her across the foyer to the glassed-in case that protected an opened, brightly illustrated book. He said, "It looks quite ancient."

She braced a gloved palm on the display case and peered down through the glass. "One can almost see the monk hunched over, dipping his brush in the brilliant colors."

"Beatrice, you're positive that you do not mind waiting here unescorted?"

"Of course not. You won't be long. This will keep me wonderfully entertained. I adore translating Latin."

She scarcely noticed when he left, but his sudden absence felt tangible. She glanced back at his swift crossing of the vestibule and his going up the staircase two steps at a time. The exquisite perfection of the religious tome in the display case recaptured her attention, until she sensed a presence standing near. She shifted sideways to allow someone else an unobstructed view.

A male voice from behind said, "Extraordinary workmanship, is it not?"

She kept reading. "Yes."

"It's on loan to the institute. A privately-owned piece."

She hummed a reply then looked up when she felt his presence move closer. She glanced over her shoulder and saw a rather dashing gentleman. He removed his hat, revealing black hair sleekly curled. She tempered cringing recoil when his gaze gleamed with too much appreciation. She wasn't accustomed to gentlemen making their admiration known.

When she shifted sideways, he took her hand and bowed. "Captain Langston Blake at your service, ma'am."

She said the first thing that came into her head. "I'm waiting for my husband."

"Of course, you are. So many husbands are in favor of furthering their wife's educations. Quite modern of them."

She didn't care for his innuendo that she'd invented a prevarication to discourage him and tugged free the hand that he hadn't released. "Sir, we've not been introduced."

"I just told you my name. May I have the pleasure of knowing yours?"

She gave him her most severe expression of disapproval. "Sir, I am countrified but not a fool. I cannot believe that universally established rules of conduct might be suspended in London. I've made it clear that I do not know you. Please, go away."

He replaced his hat and firmly took her arm. "Allow me to lead you away from the entrance. So many people coming and going. A lady should not be unaccompanied in public. It leads to the wrong impression."

She pointedly looked down at the hand that encircled her arm then back up at him with a warning squint. Before she could kick his booted shin, a tall figure stepped between them.

Joss said in a low, ugly voice she didn't recognize, "Take your hand off her before I hack it off."

Captain Blake immediately let go of her arm and retreated a step. "Good day to you, Warfield. I was merely escorting the lady to somewhere less public."

"Keeping in mind your reputation, Blake, I'm not surprised that you tried. This is my wife, and you are leaving."

Blake replaced his hat, walked the few steps to the entrance, and exited. Beatrice glared at his back and wished she were allowed to call out something inappropriate. After the tittle-tattle she'd created from unintentionally snubbing Lady Alis, she kept that wish to herself. There were too many people milling about.

Joss handed her the reticule. A light touch on her back directed her out onto Albermarle Street where he glared at Captain Blake stepping up into a hackney. Watching as the hackney moved out into the traffic, he muttered a few of the epithets she wished she had the luxury of venting. He curtly nodded to a waiting groom, and the lad trotted off to find their town coach.

Joss refused to let his horses stand for long periods of time, and at intervals, had them walked up and down the busy thoroughfare.

While they waited for the coach, he attempted to put the incident behind them with a forced conversation but continued to look distracted. He finally asked, "Did you enjoy the lecture?"

"Not my particular field of interest but there was much to be learned. I have so little understanding of the sciences. There was another woman in the audience, which surprised me."

"Yes. The baroness is not a favorite, therefore you were not as remarked upon. Were you uncomfortable with the lack of women present?"

The coach pulled up just then and the groom opened the door and let down the steps. She waited to answer until they were settled and the carriage moving.

"I had resolved myself long ago to become accustomed to my oddities. The only discomfort was when you told Captain Blake that you might remove his arm. I believe your exact wording was that you would hack it off. That was a bit…unusual."

Joss directed his attention to the traffic as the coach turned onto Park Lane. "I apologize for that. Blake has an excessively unsavory reputation for taking advantage. And I was not pleased with myself for leaving you unattended."

"I had no qualms. Surely a woman is safe standing in the vestibule at the Royal Institute."

"Generally speaking, yes, but a bounder like Blake has no reservations. Perhaps I spoke somewhat rashly."

Due to the subtle chill in his voice, she elected to let the matter drop but couldn't stop thinking about it.

134

The violence of his reaction was distressing. Being a part of an almost altercation rendered her confused for many reasons. Her husband's behavior indicated possessiveness as well as protectiveness. Perhaps even jealousy?

She'd never considered herself much of a catch. And at her age, certainly not a candidate for the first bench at a Bath assembly, where the prime pickings on the marriage mart were ceremoniously seated. The older ladies at home had talked endlessly about husband hunting and all their beaus. Even if just coming out, Beatrice wasn't the sort to inspire poetry, as Joss had made a point of telling her at Asterly House. Another fiasco and today's makes two.

There was some comfort in knowing that she wasn't entirely without beaus. She'd received a number of proposals. True, they were men strongly encouraged to do so by others. None had much interest in her and were undoubtedly appalled at the idea of marrying an educated female, one far more intelligent and well read than they. Her only bona fide proposal had come on the heels of a social gaffe—a pre-London fiasco. Joss, being the rigidly conventional fellow he was, made a chivalrous offer that he later described as one of convenience, which left little to boost the measurement as to how she was valued by men.

There was the aspect of protecting what was one's own, and perhaps that was the root reason for provoking such a startling response from Joss at the institute. In his point of view, a man would rush to protect his family.

Her thoughts kept returning to the extremity of his response on the verge of menace. Strangely, his ferocity hadn't frightened her, but no matter how she viewed it, his actions appeared too forceful, unnecessarily so. She would never outright express that opinion, because that would lead to thinking that he was acting possessively. That required review, but it was becoming difficult to remove her feelings, to step back for an unbiased assessment.

How did she feel about being relegated to a nonentity, a piece of property, merely a possession to protect, a comparison similar to a dog growling over a bone? Was that so lowering after all? It might mean that Joss thought more of her than merely a practical end to the problem of procreation to continue the line.

A dark weight spread throughout her chest, squeezing her heart. If Joss saw her as merely an expedient resolution to both of their problems, would she ever experience the bliss Emily alluded to when she spoke of the marriage bed? According to Emily, after the initial discomfort of the initiation, pleasure indescribable followed. She supposed that must be true. There had to be some reason for so much written about it through the ages.

She sneaked a peripheral peek at Joss. He continued to glare at the view of Hyde Park passing by the windows, face fixed in stern lines. Perhaps he was regretting that he'd ever married her. He must be making comparisons. He might be wishing he were in the company of a more entertaining lady, one more charming, with easy graces and not with a head filled with learning.

A stinging sensation pricked her eyes. She forced down a swallow and blinked rapidly, fighting to calm and conceal flying emotions. Joss had an uncanny way of perceiving her feelings and proved this when he shifted his attention away from the window to her.

"Beatrice, is something amiss?"

How did he do that, always intuiting her distress? Drat the man. "Tis nothing. A cinder."

As she fumbled with her reticule for a handkerchief, he ordered the coach to stop and switched to the forward seat. He shook out his handkerchief as he sat next to her.

Cupping her chin, he ordered, "Look up."

She focused on keeping her chin from trembling by studying the edge of his hat's curled brim, which he removed suddenly when he became impatient with it hampering a closer inspection.

"Let's try this again. Look up. That's it. Hmm. I don't see anything. Perhaps you blinked it free."

She nodded slightly in his light grasp. He didn't move. She concentrated on not cringing away from his intense examination. His scent, clean with a hint of cologne and something of himself filled her head.

"Beatrice, open your eyes."

When she did, she couldn't look directly at him and stared at the coach's ceiling. Her heart did a little twist when he released her and shifted back to his seat. Her thanks sounded congested. She'd barely gotten the words out of a throat so tight she could scarcely breathe.

He looked out the window again, away from her, his expression harsh and unhappy, most likely ruing a marriage to an unsophisticated country girl. She didn't know how to rectify this, his coldness, the estrangement. If she had a book or a friend to guide her, she might find the courage to attempt to break through

137

his defensive shell. There were words she wanted to say, emotions trapped inside her chest. Her lack of understanding of how to address matters of intimacy with her husband pulled her gaze from his sullen mood to the view out of the opposite window. Perhaps she could write to Emily, ask in veiled terms what could be done and how to demolish the wall that grew higher and more dense with every day that passed.

Chapter 16

Joss had been unable to eat dinner, sensitive to Beatrice's sadness throughout a meal where she also couldn't eat and pushed food around her plate. She excused herself early, claiming weariness when they were both aware of her sturdy, country girl constitution. Unable to read or get clear of his mood, he went up to bed.

He scarcely noticed Cervantes peeling the jacket from his back and arms. The cloth tied around his neck choked, and Joss couldn't get it unknotted fast enough. Even after flinging it aside he still felt throttled. The ugly memory of Langston Blake's greasy sneer refused to fade. No amount of forcing it from his mind worked, nor the memory of Bea's affronted expression, her confusion with what the bounder was about. Part of his fury was tangled up with his frustration with the way her mind worked. He couldn't get past her persistent belief that she held no allure for any male. The memory of the brute imposing himself on Bea sent a fresh rush of outrage surging through his veins.

Take your hand off her or I'll hack it off.

Had he really said that out loud? He needed to be alone to wrestle with his mood, the liquid, rippling river of outrage that howled in his veins. After Cervantes carefully removed the snug-fitting boots, Joss dismissed him for the night. Tugging free the hem of his shirt from his breeches, he paced the room, trying to wear down emotions boiling inside. It wasn't jealousy. It was protective rage, something he'd never felt before to this degree, and its violence was an enlightening surprise.

He'd never been emotionally undisciplined. Such behavior simply was not done in public. His father had never allowed his sons to show any outward emotion. Part of Bea's attractiveness was her openness. One of his hopes had been that marriage to her, being around her natural spontaneity, would lighten his difficulty with self-expression. In moderation, of course, nothing too outré.

This relentless agitation, the roiling need to smash something, preferably Blake's face, was as unsettling as it was annoying. Pacing the confines of the bedroom didn't help. Ramming a fist into the bounder's nose would have relieved some of the scorching anger but would have caused a social upheaval of gigantic proportions. A fist-fight in the lobby of the Royal Institute? Such an incident would connect Bea's name to one of the vilest men in town. A scandal beyond anything—a streaming scream of gossip that would blaze across the city faster than fire—one his pragmatic wife would shrug off. He wouldn't allow it, couldn't bear the idea of it for her sake. Blake was the sort who liked to boast of his conquests. It was pretty much taken for granted that most of what he said were lies. That would make no difference to the abundance of vitriol, the spreading of the falsehood connected to Bea. His blood was up and the struggle to quiet it wasn't helped by pacing or thinking about it over and over, imagining alternate scenes.

He stopped pacing and inhaled deep, calming breaths then sat on the windowsill. Looking out at the moon on the river, he tried to clear his mind of useless anger. The event was over. He wouldn't call the man out and risk smudging Bea's name with any hint of association with Langston Blake's.

Moonlight wavered a long trail of shimmering light on black river water. He took another deep breath. When had this happened, this obsessive fascination for a staid bluestocking? Mistresses and affairs had come and gone over the years, some more satisfying than others. The element of risk, the possibility of scandal or being caught-out by a husband had played its part when he was young. Those days were long-past dead. In recent years the libidinous rendezvous felt tedious, the stimulation of the chase gone off. So what was it about prim do-gooder Beatrice Allardyce Warfield that made him lose all sense?

Chaotic memories stopped on the recollection of the Asterly party, when he'd stopped her talking with a kiss. Before they married, he'd meant it when he had assured her that he had no problem with waiting to set up their nursery. That was before he kissed her. After that, denials and roadblocks got torn aside. There was no masking the fact that she knew nothing about lovemaking, was utterly innocent and yet curious and receptive. She was no longer a girl. She must know the mechanics, or did she? She hadn't resisted, but hadn't participated, while he'd been jolted to the core by her wide-eyed puzzlement. She appeared to have no idea that it took all of his discipline not to grab her by the hair and fling her onto the nearest surface. His wife. What the bloody hell was wrong with him?

He ignored the scratching on the door until the snap of the latch made him flinch. He'd wanted to deny that the source came from the dressing room that connected their apartments. His heart sank then started to pound when Beatrice came out of the shadows and hesitantly stepped into the room.

"I'm sorry. I didn't mean to disturb—"

"Not at all. What is it?"

She stared, and he remembered that he was half-dressed, his shirt hanging open, feet bare and breeches partially undone. A spear of heat sliced through him when she nervously licked her lips. Her eyes gleamed, anxious.

She came closer, into the faint light from a lamp lit by the bed. She paused when he stood and stepped away from the windowsill. The cauldron of emotions whirling inside settled, solidifying into a knot deep and low from the sight, the nearness of what he wanted. She wore a thin dressing robe loosely tied. Fragile lace encircled the nightgown buttoned up to her throat. He'd seen many provocatively dressed and undressed women but none had affected him like Beatrice with her honest gaze and intrepid integrity. All the bottled anger at Langston Blake, himself and revolting gossipmongers veered, changing direction, hardening into something not pleasant.

What was it about this woman that made him lose his grip on common sense? Hair the color of honey streaked with sunlight hung down her back in soft waves. Her wide gaze glistened with concern that made him edgy. Why must she be so oblivious to what her presence in his rooms late at night must provoke?

She attempted a smile that came and went too
142

quickly. Her eyes widened when he moved closer, her voice gruff when she said, "I have been concerned and thinking a great deal about what happened today at the Royal Institute."

"What about it?" Blast it. That had come out mean sounding.

She fussed with the end of the night robe's sash. "Well, you were decidedly unhappy, and never said much in regards to the incident. Afterwards, I mean."

Looking panicky, she forced down a swallow before saying, "I do hope that I didn't give the impression that I encouraged that horrid man in any way. You didn't think that, did you?"

She winced when he snapped out, "Don't be ridiculous." Feeling like a cad, he attempted to gentle his tone. "You haven't a flirtatious bone in your body, and Blake is a known bounder."

"I see. Forgive me, but I never imagined you for a man plagued by sudden emotional responses. You do have a reputation—"

"And what do you mean by that?"

There it was, that defiant tilt of her chin. "Well, you cannot deny that a particular status, certain events in your past were widely circulated."

"Madam, I have never accosted an unattended female and never would."

"I'm not suggesting—"

"Precisely what part of my past has you thinking you might compare me to a lout like Langston Blake?"

"Not like him, precisely, but there are rumors—"

"What rumors?"

"That of you and ladies of the ton. Widows and married women of easy virtue. Wives of friends—"

"I would never form a liaison with a friend's wife. You insult me, madam, without cause. I am no saint but that particular sin against a friend is not mine."

His heart pinched when her expression tightened with worry and shame, but a wilder feeling spurred him on, made him want to lash out. "Perhaps if I had a wife with a portion of the compassion she so freely offers to others I might not be out-countenanced by your saintly perfection. Hail holy Lady Warfield, who forgives a whoring rake before her own blameless husband."

Before he could apologize for the harshness of his reaction, her expression shattered. She mumbled something and fled. Anger at himself for an unreasonable attack and her sudden flight spurred the baser need to chase. Cursing his darker self, he followed her through the dressing room and sitting room and flung open her bedchamber door. His blood up and raging, he barely noticed the widening of her eyes. She stood by the bed in her nightgown. The dressing robe slipped from her fingers as she stared. For an endless moment, they shared a visual understanding.

"I see that it's time," she whispered.

He took that as permission and strode across the room. The delicate lawn of her nightwear felt clean and fragile as he grasped the material and gathered it up. The soft skin of her waist, so narrow his fingers almost touched, ripped away what was left of his control. The ardor he'd held in check, the yearning long denied. He lifted her onto the bed. His trembling fingers tore at the resistive buttons on his breeches. Her softness was finally under him, in his hands, his Bea, his wife. Joy and pleasure poured out in a blur, a release so blinding

144

and sudden that afterward all he heard was the sounds of his rasping breath and a strangely empty relief.

Reality, what he'd done came at him like a physical blow. Appalled, he looked down at Beatrice lying so still and quiet beneath him, her stunned, unblinking stare into the shadowy room, not at him. Her head was turned slightly to one side on the pillow from his grip on a handful of silky hair. He immediately released her.

Humiliation sank into every cell of his being when he realized what he'd done. He hadn't even removed his britches, just yanked open the buttons and fell on her.

She winced as he carefully withdrew. He gently eased off and away from her warmth and softness. Standing beside the bed, he was unable to look away from gown he'd shoved up to her throat, the whiteness of her skin, the slimness of her legs, the brutish mess he'd wrought. Under the hem of his shirt, he fastened the buttons he'd hadn't torn off. Raging emotion had cooled to self-loathing with the proof he'd become the creature he'd accused Blake of being, the lesser being his wife assumed her husband was.

Sounding dazed and yet with her peculiar way of being intrigued by the new and unusual, she murmured to the shadows of the canopy overhead, "That wasn't quite what one expected."

Stung by all that could mean for their future together, hurt blurted a harsh reply. "So sorry to have disappointed, madam."

She angled her head on the pillow in his direction He could tell by the distance in her gaze that she was still preoccupied with inner examination. "You're not

145

to worry. It's only that I was led to believe this event would be quite different."

Shame and nausea had him grabbing the bedcovers and flinging them over the evidence of his dishonorable behavior. That unfortunately took her attention from introspection to him.

Before she could say more that would surely lacerate his soul, he ground out, "Be assured that I will not inconvenience you every night. There are mistresses for that."

He managed not to slam the bedchamber door when he fled. He got to the threshold of his bedroom and stumbled against the doorway. With a sob, he rammed the side of his fist against the wall, pressed his forehead into it, and struggled to contain the convulsive need to weep.

Why had he said something so cruel, behaved so unlike himself? And why to Bea, someone he desperately loved? How could he repair this? Was what he'd done to her, to their future, repairable? Forgivable?

Straightening up, he turned to confront the door he'd just fled through. If he didn't deal with this now, a barrier could rise between them. She couldn't physically leave him. The law gave him the right to drag her back, force her to stay, but he didn't fear Bea's physical withdrawal. The unbearable thought was that he'd demolished whatever respect she'd had for him. She'd made it quite clear from the start that their marriage was one of convenience, the only logical course of action for her, but that had never been his aim. Before Asterly had pointed it out, he'd given in to the understanding that there was a reality, a truth in

146

loving someone at first sight. A smile tried to form as he remembered Bea's bottom waving back and forth as she extricated herself from the fence. She'd rescued a pig she disliked in order to come to the aid of a distressed elderly lady. Beatrice had devoted her life to her father and helping others. His Bea felt compelled to serve others much in the same way humans were compelled to breathe.

And he'd treated her worse than any woman he'd ever had relations with, behaved in a manner incomprehensible. He gathered every scrap of fortitude and courage he could dredge up from the waste of his soul. More than anything, he wanted her respect, but would settle and be grateful for forgiveness.

Joss had been unable to eat dinner, sensitive to Beatrice's sadness throughout a meal where she also couldn't eat and pushed food around her plate. She excused herself early, claiming weariness when they were both aware of her sturdy, country girl constitution. Unable to read or get clear of his mood, he went up to bed.

He scarcely noticed Cervantes peeling the jacket from his back and arms. The cloth tied around his neck choked, and Joss couldn't get it unknotted fast enough. Even after flinging it aside he still felt throttled. The ugly memory of Langston Blake's greasy sneer refused to fade. No amount of forcing it from his mind worked, nor the memory of Bea's affronted expression, her confusion with what the bounder was about. Part of his fury was tangled up with his frustration with the way her mind worked. He couldn't get past her persistent belief that she held no allure for any male. The memory of the brute imposing himself on Bea sent a fresh rush of outrage surging through his veins.

Take your hand off her or I'll hack it off.

Had he really said that out loud? He needed to be alone to wrestle with his mood, the liquid, rippling river of outrage that howled in his veins. After Cervantes carefully removed the snug-fitting boots, Joss dismissed him for the night. Tugging free the hem of his shirt from his breeches, he paced the room, trying to wear down emotions boiling inside. It wasn't jealousy. It was protective rage, something he'd never felt before to this degree, and its violence was an enlightening surprise.

He'd never been emotionally undisciplined. Such behavior simply was not done in public. His father had never allowed his sons to show any outward emotion. Part of Bea's attractiveness was her openness. One of his hopes had been that marriage to her, being around her natural spontaneity, would lighten his difficulty with self-expression. In moderation, of course, nothing too outré.

This relentless agitation, the roiling need to smash something, preferably Blake's face, was as unsettling as it was annoying. Pacing the confines of the bedroom didn't help. Ramming a fist into the bounder's nose would have relieved some of the scorching anger but would have caused a social upheaval of gigantic proportions. A fist-fight in the lobby of the Royal Institute? Such an incident would connect Bea's name to one of the vilest men in town. A scandal beyond anything—a streaming scream of gossip that would blaze across the city faster than fire—one his pragmatic wife would shrug off. He wouldn't allow it, couldn't bear the idea of it for her sake. Blake was the sort who

148

liked to boast of his conquests. It was pretty much taken for granted that most of what he said were lies. That would make no difference to the abundance of vitriol, the spreading of the falsehood connected to Bea. His blood was up and the struggle to quiet it wasn't helped by pacing or thinking about it over and over, imagining alternate scenes.

He stopped pacing and inhaled deep, calming breaths then sat on the windowsill. Looking out at the moon on the river, he tried to clear his mind of useless anger. The event was over. He wouldn't call the man out and risk smudging Bea's name with any hint of association with Langston Blake's.

Moonlight wavered a long trail of shimmering light on black river water. He took another deep breath. When had this happened, this obsessive fascination for a staid bluestocking? Mistresses and affairs had come and gone over the years, some more satisfying than others. The element of risk, the possibility of scandal or being caught-out by a husband had played its part when he was young. Those days were long-past dead. In recent years the libidinous rendezvous felt tedious, the stimulation of the chase gone off. So what was it about prim do-gooder Beatrice Allardyce Warfield that made him lose all sense?

Chaotic memories stopped on the recollection of the Asterly party, when he'd stopped her talking with a kiss. Before they married, he'd meant it when he had assured her that he had no problem with waiting to set up their nursery. That was before he kissed her. After that, denials and roadblocks got torn aside. There was no masking the fact that she knew nothing about lovemaking, was utterly innocent and yet curious and receptive. She was no longer a girl. She must know the mechanics, or did she? She hadn't resisted, but hadn't participated, while he'd been jolted to the core by her wide-eyed puzzlement. She appeared to have no idea that it took all of his discipline not to grab her by the hair and fling her onto the nearest surface. His wife. What the bloody hell was wrong with him?

He ignored the scratching on the door until the snap of the latch made him flinch. He'd wanted to deny that the source came from the dressing room that connected their apartments. His heart sank then started to pound when Beatrice came out of the shadows and hesitantly stepped into the room.

"I'm sorry. I didn't mean to disturb—"

"Not at all. What is it?"

She stared, and he remembered that he was half-dressed, his shirt hanging open, feet bare and breeches partially undone. A spear of heat sliced through him when she nervously licked her lips. Her eyes gleamed, anxious.

She came closer, into the faint light from a lamp lit by the bed. She paused when he stood and stepped away from the windowsill. The cauldron of emotions whirling inside settled, solidifying into a knot deep and low from the sight, the nearness of what he wanted. She wore a thin dressing robe loosely tied. Fragile lace encircled the nightgown buttoned up to her throat. He'd seen many provocatively dressed and undressed women but none had affected him like Beatrice with her honest gaze and intrepid integrity. All the bottled anger at Langston Blake, himself and revolting gossipmongers veered, changing direction, hardening into something not pleasant.

What was it about this woman that made him lose his grip on common sense? Hair the color of honey streaked with sunlight hung down her back in soft waves. Her wide gaze glistened with concern that made him edgy. Why must she be so oblivious to what her presence in his rooms late at night must provoke?

She attempted a smile that came and went too quickly. Her eyes widened when he moved closer, her voice gruff when she said, "I have been concerned and thinking a great deal about what happened today at the Royal Institute."

"What about it?" Blast it. That had come out mean sounding.

She fussed with the end of the night robe's sash. "Well, you were decidedly unhappy, and never said much in regards to the incident. Afterwards, I mean."

Looking panicky, she forced down a swallow before saying, "I do hope that I didn't give the impression that I encouraged that horrid man in any way. You didn't think that, did you?"

She winced when he snapped out, "Don't be ridiculous." Feeling like a cad, he attempted to gentle his tone. "You haven't a flirtatious bone in your body, and Blake is a known bounder."

"I see. Forgive me, but I never imagined you for a man plagued by sudden emotional responses. You do have a reputation—"

"And what do you mean by that?"

There it was, that defiant tilt of her chin. "Well, you cannot deny that a particular status, certain events in your past were widely circulated."

"Madam, I have never accosted an unattended female and never would."

151

"I'm not suggesting—"

"Precisely what part of my past has you thinking you might compare me to a lout like Langston Blake?"

"Not like him, precisely, but there are rumors—"

"What rumors?"

"That of you and ladies of the ton. Widows and married women of easy virtue. Wives of friends—"

"I would never form a liaison with a friend's wife. You insult me, madam, without cause. I am no saint but that particular sin against a friend is not mine."

His heart pinched when her expression tightened with worry and shame, but a wilder feeling spurred him on, made him want to lash out. "Perhaps if I had a wife with a portion of the compassion she so freely offers to others I might not be out-countenanced by your saintly perfection. Hail holy Lady Warfield, who forgives a whoring rake before her own blameless husband."

Before he could apologize for the harshness of his reaction, her expression shattered. She mumbled something and fled. Anger at himself for an unreasonable attack and her sudden flight spurred the baser need to chase. Cursing his darker self, he followed her through the dressing room and sitting room and flung open her bedchamber door. His blood up and raging, he barely noticed the widening of her eyes. She stood by the bed in her nightgown. The dressing robe slipped from her fingers as she stared. For an endless moment, they shared a visual understanding.

"I see that it's time," she whispered.

He took that as permission and strode across the room. The delicate lawn of her nightwear felt clean and fragile as he grasped the material and gathered it up.

152

The soft skin of her waist, so narrow his fingers almost touched, ripped away what was left of his control. The ardor he'd held in check, the yearning long denied. He lifted her onto the bed. His trembling fingers tore at the resistive buttons on his breeches. Her softness was finally under him, in his hands, his Bea, his wife. Joy and pleasure poured out in a blur, a release so blinding and sudden that afterward all he heard was the sounds of his rasping breath and a strangely empty relief.

Reality, what he'd done came at him like a physical blow. Appalled, he looked down at Beatrice lying so still and quiet beneath him, her stunned, unblinking stare into the shadowy room, not at him. Her head was turned slightly to one side on the pillow from his grip on a handful of silky hair. He immediately released her.

Humiliation sank into every cell of his being when he realized what he'd done. He hadn't even removed his britches, just yanked open the buttons and fell on her.

She winced as he carefully withdrew. He gently eased off and away from her warmth and softness. Standing beside the bed, he was unable to look away from gown he'd shoved up to her throat, the whiteness of her skin, the slimness of her legs, the brutish mess he'd wrought. Under the hem of his shirt, he fastened the buttons he'd hadn't torn off. Raging emotion had cooled to self-loathing with the proof he'd become the creature he'd accused Blake of being, the lesser being his wife assumed her husband was.

Sounding dazed and yet with her peculiar way of being intrigued by the new and unusual, she murmured to the shadows of the canopy overhead, "That wasn't

153

quite what one expected."

Stung by all that could mean for their future together, hurt blurted a harsh reply. "So sorry to have disappointed, madam."

She angled her head on the pillow in his direction He could tell by the distance in her gaze that she was still preoccupied with inner examination. "You're not to worry. It's only that I was led to believe this event would be quite different."

Shame and nausea had him grabbing the bedcovers and flinging them over the evidence of his dishonorable behavior. That unfortunately took her attention from introspection to him.

Before she could say more that would surely lacerate his soul, he ground out, "Be assured that I will not inconvenience you every night. There are mistresses for that."

He managed not to slam the bedchamber door when he fled. He got to the threshold of his bedroom and stumbled against the doorway. With a sob, he rammed the side of his fist against the wall, pressed his forehead into it, and struggled to contain the convulsive need to weep.

Why had he said something so cruel, behaved so unlike himself? And why to Bea, someone he desperately loved? How could he repair this? Was what he'd done to her, to their future, repairable? Forgivable?

Straightening up, he turned to confront the door he'd just fled through. If he didn't deal with this now, a barrier could rise between them. She couldn't physically leave him. The law gave him the right to drag her back, force her to stay, but he didn't fear Bea's physical withdrawal. The unbearable thought was that he'd demolished whatever respect she'd had for him. She'd made it quite clear from the start that their marriage was one of convenience, the only logical course of action for her, but that had never been his aim. Before Asterly had pointed it out, he'd given in to the understanding that there was a reality, a truth in loving someone at first sight. A smile tried to form as he remembered Bea's bottom waving back and forth as she extricated herself from the fence. She'd rescued a pig she disliked in order to come to the aid of a distressed elderly lady. Beatrice had devoted her life to her father and helping others. His Bea felt compelled to serve others much in the same way humans were compelled to breathe.

And he'd treated her worse than any woman he'd ever had relations with, behaved in a manner incomprehensible. He gathered every scrap of fortitude and courage he could dredge up from the waste of his soul. More than anything, he wanted her respect, but would settle and be grateful for forgiveness.

Chapter 17

She'd thought it would sting when she washed away the wet between her legs, but the cool water felt soothing. A light smearing of blood tinted the water left in the bowl from evening ablutions. She froze when the bedchamber door clicked opened. She watched, half-bent over, as he crossed the room. It wasn't until he gently removed the damp cloth from her fingers that she remembered that she'd left her nightgown on the bed.

The embarrassing smear of blood on the cloth prompted an urgent explanation. "I'm sorry. I hadn't realized that I'd started my courses."

He shook his head and dropped the cloth in the bowl. With a tenderness that shattered her heart, he leaned down and lifted her up in his arms. "No, dearest, that's what happens the first time."

It felt so wonderful to be carried that she rested her cheek on his shoulder. He surprised her when he didn't lay her on the bed, but sat on its edge and held her on his lap. It felt odd to be without clothes while he was almost fully dressed, but wonderful. She dared to place her hand on his chest to feel the warmth and texture of his skin. The bedside candles she hadn't snuffed allowed enough light to watch as her thumb rubbed lightly over hair that felt coarser than that on his head.

"Are you all right, Beatrice?"

"Of course. I am a bit worried."

"Can you tell me why?"

"You see, it was explained to me that conception never happens when a woman is on her courses. I didn't want you disappointed that the effort was for naught."

An odd sound, a catch in his voice lifted her head from his shoulder. "What is it? Have I done or said something I shouldn't?"

He was looking up at the ceiling, so she couldn't see his face. He said in a choked-up voice, "Stop, Beatrice. Please!"

She relented, looking back at the little she could see of his exposed skin between his parted shirt. He was so much more interesting than Sir Harry. And there was something about his scent that made it impossible not to nuzzle her nose against him and inhale his essence.

She felt her eyes widened when he gathered her closer and pressed his face into her hair with a soft moan. She really should have braided it, rather than let it hang everywhere in a mess.

He relaxed his tight hold. "Beatrice, will you look at me? What I did before, my behavior tonight was inexcusable. I ask your forgiveness and promise that it will never be like that again."

"It was a bit different from what I'd been led to expect. According to Emily. And I shouldn't blame you if I am such a disappointment that you should feel compelled to find…affection elsewhere."

"You must stop. Please, Bea! There will never be anyone else. I spoke rashly. You are in no way at fault.

157

I acted in the most brutish way possible. Will you let me make amends?"

"Certainly. And there is nothing to forgive. I pledged a duty, and I am fully sensible that my responsibility is to provide an heir. And most grateful. You have given me a lovely room where I can write or read or do as I please. I am quite content but must ask that you feel no obligation. Isn't it my obligation to submit?"

She felt his shoulders sag. "Bea, you unman me."

"Oh, I shouldn't think that a good thing. Even though it hurt a bit, perhaps we should explore our duty again?"

After a gentle kiss, which made her wish he'd do the open-mouthed version, he laid her on the bed. She was glad she'd lit more candles to bathe when he began to undress, dropping clothes on the floor. She forgot to reprimand such untidiness when he stretched out beside her, warm, solid and so much larger, but not in a way that frightened. Her pulse sped up in a pleasant way with the anticipation that she might again get to witness a man in full arousal. His vigorous taking of her body had been wonderfully exciting. She'd never dreamed that Joss would want her physically or come to her in such a state of relentless passion.

What he was doing now wiped away the exciting image of his earlier behavior, when he was so gripped by passion that he didn't take time to disrobe. Tender, gliding touches now made her gasp. Enthralled by his gentle coaxing, she felt her body lift and move with his guidance. The grazing glide of fingertips sent quivers over her skin. The startling use of his lips and tongue induced groans that excited him, caused him to tense and quiver. Whispered instructions gave her confidence to respond. There were gentle bites on her lips and elsewhere. The shock of his mouth where it shouldn't be made an unfamiliar being within her cry out, beg for more. Spiraling need wound her body tighter, straining for something unknown, out of reach, on the edge. His guiding hands made her frantic, showed her where to touch him, how to hold him with arms and legs, until the slow stroking had her moaning, sobbing. The night sank into a well of pleasure she never wanted to leave.

So this was what they wrote about, hinted at, this escape to a place where there was a love that which she now feared to lose. Against her ear, she heard loving whispers, endearments, encouragement. This time his completion sounded gentler, not an agonizing outcry of release, but the sweet groan of transcendence, everything Emily had promised, but so much better, and as she'd said, indescribable.

Sleep came suddenly in the safety of his arms, but he was gone when she awoke. Morning's murky light seeped through a gap in the curtains. With increasing awareness, she remembered the night before. She carefully itemized the differences in her body, another kind of awareness. There were tender spots and vague aches in unexpected places that renewed the pleasures of all he'd taught her. Even though it had been the first time, the initiation hadn't been as horrible as he'd thought it had been for her. The second and third times had been revelations. She now truly belonged to him and he to her. Careful review unveiled the discovery that with physical relations came the emotional. There had been whispers in the dark, some urgent, others the beginnings of honest admissions. She'd lost her awe of him with his confession that he thought she nourished a poor opinion of him. That astounded and made her think about being more circumspect in how she spoke to him and to others.

She hadn't realized that she'd fallen in love. She'd vowed during the wedding ceremony to love her husband. Nowhere was it written that she had to be in love with him. Somewhere along the way, perhaps her initiation last night into bodily passion, the scale had tipped. She'd moved beyond respecting the unapproachable Sir Jocelyn to falling headlong for the earthy and very *un*-urbane Joss. A grin twitched her lips. She softly chuckled, rolled onto her back, and stretched luxuriously. Some things were better, vastly more delicious, when served up raw.

Chapter 18

The rising sun glowed gold and pink through the morning haze. Beatrice idly brushed the tapered end of the feather quill across her chin. She'd sharpened the tip earlier but hadn't written anything. The restful view from her desk in front of the window absorbed all creativity. The lawn stretched down to the Thames. As much as she loved the country, waking to this scene every morning had become an unexpected blessing.

Recollections of her initiation into what the marriage bed involved also had a part in the disinclination to write or to do anything but remember the night before. This morning a different kind of hunger had taken hold, making her wonder how long she'd have to wait for more lessons that only a husband could instruct.

A tap on the door broke into peaceful thoughts, memories, and grateful prayers. Joss partially opened the dressing room door that separated her rooms from his.

"Good morning, Beatrice. May I come in?"

"Certainly." She set down the quill, closed the inkwell lid, and stood.

He only took a few steps into the room. He was dressed casually, half-boots and black pantaloons, bottle green jacket and shirt undone. Since she always woke with the dawn, she was fully dressed but had left her hair in its single braid.

"I beg pardon for disturbing you so early. Should I wait until you call for your maid?"

"Thank you, no. I prefer not to have her come up until I ring."

"I see," he murmured, looking uncomfortable.

"May I ask why you knocked?"

"I was wondering if you would like to join me. Punting. I often go out for a row on the river before the traffic begins."

Excitement bloomed in her chest. "Rowing? Out on the Thames? Why that sounds delightful."

His shoulders relaxed and he exhaled a pent-up breath. She'd noticed that he wasn't his usual self but hadn't realized that he was nervous. His casual attire distracted and brought reminders of the night before.

A brief smile lit his eyes. "It's damp out on the water this early. You will want a warm shawl."

She nodded and went swiftly to a chest of drawers and lifted out a woolen shawl. A wide-brimmed chip-straw hat hung inside the wardrobe. He waited for her on the threshold of the door to the passageway. They silently went down to the ground floor, through the morning room to exit through its garden door.

He asked, "The grass is wet. Do you mind it ruining your shoes?"

"These are for walking. I had planned to investigate the copse after breakfast,"

They said nothing else until they reached the river's edge. He held her arm as they crossed the narrow dock. The punt moored at its end was more luxurious that she expected. She'd envisioned a plain, small boat with wooden seats. This one had two, padded seats and a pillow-strewn chaise on the prow.

He stepped down into the boat and held up his hand for her. She settled on the soft chaise and tied the ends of the shawl. It felt cooler on the water.

As he untied tethering lines, he said, not looking at her, "If your shoes are wet, you might want to take them off to dry. There's a lap robe folded beside your seat."

She leaned over to unlace her shoes, then unfolded the robe and draped it over her lap as she settled back. "This is positively luxurious. I feel quiet decadent, sir."

He smiled and dipped the oars into the river. In a few, pulling strokes, he had the skiff centered and moving upriver. The plunk and swish of the oars and bird calls were the only sounds to interrupt the peaceful silence. She averted her gaze from the sight of his strong, stroking rhythm. His dark hair, always so perfectly brushed, now fell in waves over his forehead. The crisp white of his shirt began to wilt. The sight was one of overwhelming masculinity, unsettling, and difficult to watch without blushing.

She leaned sideways to touch the river and studied the v-shaped ripples fanning away from her fingers. "I have no idea how far we've traveled. Are you tired?"

"Only a little. It's been about two miles. Another two, I should think, and then the easy glide downriver to home."

"You aren't even out of breath."

"Not for another mile. I rowed every day when we lived here. I'm out of condition. Apologies, but I'm going to have to take off my coat now that the sun is up."

He brought up the oars into the punt to remove his
163

jacket, and she quickly looked away, again disturbed by his state of undress.

Memories from the night before revolved through her drifting thoughts. He did care about her as a person and liked to talk with her. If that was all they had as husband and wife, it was more than many ton marriages had. At least, that was her present understanding. If the passionate heat of the moment had allowed him to reveal himself then perhaps she would encourage him to take his responsibility to get her with child more frequently. If he wouldn't mind. She wasn't quite ready to suggest that. To avoid thinking how to go about that tricky problem, she turned her attention on the view. So lovely. Peaceful. Houses came and went through the trees, gliding by.

"It must have been wonderful growing up on the river for you and your brothers."

"Never did spend time with them. They were much older and off at school. I spent my time with Mother after Father died. She loved spending time on the water."

"Will you tell me about her?"

"Give me a moment. I'm going to turn us around and float us downriver."

Once the oars were at rest, he pulled off his gloves and swiped a sleeve across his forehead. His complexion was attractively flushed from exertion. She couldn't imagine rowing this heavy boat for more than a few strokes, if she could manage that.

He puffed out a few breaths and leaned forward to prop his forearms on his knees. He turned his head away to watch the slow passage of the scenery as he spoke.

"My mother married when she was fifteen. She was Father's second wife, and he, much older. I suppose he thought a young girl would fare better at giving him sons, and Mother did just that. Besides my three brothers, two more boys were stillborn.

"She wasn't a well person. Frail and often trembling when she walked. As soon as I was old enough to do so, I carried her down here. Took her rowing whenever we stayed here and the weather permitted. She said the river gave her solace."

"Has she been gone a long time?"

"Over a decade. She fortunately did not live long enough to suffer the loss of all of her sons. Howard, my oldest brother at Talavera. Next was James, the Naval contingent, at Trafalgar, and Edward of dysentery on the march in Portugal."

"So she is in heaven, waiting for her last and favorite son. Knowing she will be there to greet you is a small comfort, but it's never easy losing a parent when one is particularly close."

"We were, but I had her longer than you had yours. You were only nine. What do you remember about your mother?"

"Her disappointments."

He loosened the laces on his shirt and cooled himself by flapping the lapels. "Of what?"

"Me. She worried because I was so keen on learning. Father delighted in it, of course. Had me conversing in Greek and Latin when I should have been sewing samplers."

She looked away when he directed his gaze at her and said, "You remind me so much of her. Mother always wanted to study. Father was dead set against it.

165

I was a lad when he died and remember quite clearly how he made Mother promise not to weaken and learn to read."

"It's a disheartening fact that there are still those who consider educating females as somehow immoral. Poor Heloise, getting shuttled off to a nunnery."

She looked back at him when he said with morbid sarcasm, "Poor Abelard."

Eager to shift from the horrifying topic of Heloise's lover being castrated socially and physically, she said, "I have the impression that you read to your mother, here, on the river where no one could see."

"Yes, on the float back to Willows. Like you, she had a love for the Greeks."

"Most of the fiction is quite grisly. I admire them mainly for their innovation. And statuary. I may stand alone in the opinion that what was created in Greece should stay there and not be removed to foreign soil."

"Beatrice."

When she looked at him, she wished she hadn't. Regret looked odd on a man like Sir Jocelyn Warfield. "What is it, Joss?"

His expression lightened with a sad smile. "Do you know that's the first time you've called me that?"

"No, I hadn't. I think of you as Joss. What were you about to say?"

"You know why I brought you out on the river today?"

"I would think that you have something important to discuss and the tranquil setting might provide a balm for the unpleasant."

"Precisely. But more accurately, to ask you something."

They quietly drifted homeward. He broke the peace when he remorsefully asked, "Beatrice, will you forgive me for last night?"

Heat seared her face and she looked away. He carefully rose and stepped into the space near her feet then lowered onto the seat closest to her.

"Beatrice, what I did and said afterward…it was inexcusable. I must hope that you will forgive me."

"You are my husband. Forgiveness is expected. Even scriptural."

He gently took her hands in his. "Bea, you should know why I spoke so cruelly, behaved so inexcusably. You see, it was my pride speaking."

Pausing to assess her reaction, he smiled sadly. "Those candid blue eyes of yours are swimming in shock. But it's completely true. I've never been much concerned by how I'm viewed by others. We're alike that way, but when it comes to you, I have always sought your good favor. Last night, something about the way you spoke of your disappointment, caused the unruly side of my heart to overreact. I must again assure you that I would never seek that sort of comfort from another woman."

Her voice gruff and low, she said, "There is something to be said about repeated behaviors becoming habitual."

"Old habits, Bea." He searched her face when she averted her gaze. "What is it? If this or anything else has been troubling you, I wish you would say what is on your mind."

"Very well." She gave him a level gaze filled with challenge. "What about Elizabeth?"

"Lizzie? What about her?" When she refused to

say it and only glared, he said, "You think I had an affair with Lizzie? Whatever gave you that….ah. Lady Richardson."

"She did hint as much."

"Firstly, Lizzie is utterly unaware of other men in that way and wholly besotted with Peregrine. And the other reason, beyond the unpardonable breach of shagging your friend's wife, is that Peregrine still goes everywhere with a stiletto down the side of his boot."

"Shagging?"

"Physical relations."

"Oh, I see. But the things she implied were so appalling. I know I shouldn't have listened. I told you she was intolerable. Even more so because her attitude is that such practices are commonplace, even acceptable."

"Yes, you've heard about the adulterous ways of the ton, but I would much rather not have that sort of marriage. You've given me the impression that is also what you would want, but if it is not, and you wish to part ways after the children come, I will understand."

A spark ignited in her chest that lit a cold fire. "Sir, are you suggesting that after I have provided an heir that you would take up with other women?"

When he started to speak, but was so startled that nothing came out, she leaned forward and poked him repeatedly with a forefinger as she informed, "That. Will. Not. Happen, sir! I am your wife and you will make do with what you have. No country house parties where shooting is not the primary entertainment. No mistress tucked away on the unfashionable side of town. No becoming the ciscebo to lonely widows or ignored wives. Have I made myself understood, sir?"

He blinked and began to laugh. She narrowed her eyes threateningly but couldn't hold in the giggles bubbling up. Pressing a hand to the side of her face, she choked out, "Oh, Joss, I never knew I had that in me!"

They continued to laugh as he wobbled the boat in the process of climbing across the space to join her on the chaise.

She shrieked, "Joss, you'll overturn us! I can't swim."

"That will have to be remedied." He snuggled next to her and removed her hat, tossing it into the foot well. "And this boat is too well made to tip that easily."

Time passed. The boat drifted. Clouds floated overhead in a perfectly blue sky. She'd never dreamed that there could be so much comfort and safety in a man's embrace.

"Joss?" When he hummed a contented sounding reply, she asked, "Were there a great many women, lovers, in your past?"

"And just when I assumed we'd reached a point of sublime tranquility and understanding."

"Tell me."

"I'm not a monk, Bea." When she jiggled her shoulder against him, he said, "I'm not quite sure how to answer."

"With honesty."

He shifted to settle her more comfortably against his side and braced a boot heel against an oarlock. "To be blunt, I started quite young and it's been continuous."

"Oh."

"You sound positively defeated, my Beatrice, and shouldn't. The dreadful thing is that I have no memory

169

of most of them."

"Joss, that's terrible. Are we so insignificant as a gender?"

"I like women as a gender. Very much, in fact, but the unvarnished truth is that they never piqued my interest. Other than…whatever."

Her head felt heavy and heart a bit sad. "Then it is quite understandable why you never married before getting ensnared in my turmoil."

He sat up and took her by the shoulders to shift her to face him. "Beatrice, haven't you understood by now that I *wanted* to marry you. That I contrived and manipulated to get your consent?"

Feeling small and frail, she searched his level gaze. Tears stung behind her eyes as she whispered, "Not precisely, no."

A grim expression hardened his face and thinned his lips. The long fingers encircling her upper arms gripped tighter, gave her a tiny shake. "It wasn't your pretty bottom sticking out from that damn fence that caught my interest. It was the incredible fact that a lady would think of putting herself in so appalling a situation and all for a pig."

Mouth trembling, knowing she was on the verge of hearing a validation she longed for, she hoarsely argued, "Not for the pig. For Mrs. Pritchard."

His kiss was soft and brief. "You scowled up at me, put me in my place, argued and resisted. You helped everyone, everywhere, all of the time. I watched altruism pour out of you like nothing I'd ever seen. You are so intelligent, righteous, so pragmatic and frighteningly honest. And yet spontaneous. I needed…I *need* that. I have lived in fear of becoming my father

170

and was well on the way. You stopped me, stopped it from happening."

"Only you could do that for yourself."

"No, my Bea, you held up a mirror, and I will be honest about one thing. There is a part of my father that I will not relinquish. I keep what is mine."

"And perhaps can be somewhat…jealous?"

"Overprotective."

"I won't mind that, Joss."

"Tell me, now, that you've forgiven me?"

"For all those past indiscretions?"

"No. For being such a beast the first time last night."

"*Stoopid*, of course I have. It's not your fault if I was disappointed."

"In this case, it certainly is. I behaved horribly."

"It wasn't as terrible as you think it was. More informative and only mildly uncomfortable. Sir, there is no need for a dramatic, despairing groan for commentary. And, you came back later, quite altered, and showed me how that part of marriage can be enjoyable, exactly as Emily promised."

"There goes Lady Darcourt, again making promises that others may not be able to fulfill. I wish there were a way to scold her for giving you excessive expectations."

"She was only trying to make things easier. I had no mother to confide in or to ask questions. One gleans the basics from educational materials, of course, but I was fairly certain that the mere basics were not enough to qualify me as informed. And why are you grinning at me?"

"I adore it when you rattle on when sorting out

logic from fiction. Now that I've been forgiven and established that my appalling reaction was due to a pathetic lack of confidence—

"What are you unconfident about? No, more precisely, what could make you think you have reason for a lack of confidence for any reason?"

"Now that is an adorable reaction, spiking up like that in my defense."

"As well I should! You are my husband after all and have no reason to believe I would ever think poorly of you." After hearing herself, she amended, "In any event, no one else is allowed to say so but me."

"Beatrice, from the moment we met you made it patently obvious that whatever it is that I am, there is much to be found wanting."

"You are being ridiculous."

"Am I? I've never met a person whose esteem I wished more to possess than yours."

"Whatever for? There is so much about you that is perfect."

He stared. "Bea, have you been telling Banbury tales all this time? You've never once said anything positive. Quite often gave any indication that you felt anything other than disgust with me."

She settled back on the cushions. "You're being nonsensical. Silly."

He snuggled next to her on his side, facing her, and demanded. "Really? Then what do you actually like about me? The very first thing that struck you as positive."

"Your singing voice. It's magnificent. So lush and deep. Gives me little quivers."

She got another kind of shivery feeling when he

172

tucked his nose into the curve where her neck and shoulder met. He stopped nibbling to ask, "What else?"

"Your laugh. It's marvelous. Rolls out of you like liquid thunder. Oh, I do like what you're doing. Now I completely understand what Emily was raving about."

"Oh, my pretty Bea, there is so much for you to learn from me, and I from you, and we have previously established without question how much you like to learn."

Breathless, she clutched his shirt then released the cloth to slide her hand inside over taut, damp skin. When he hummed approval, low and deep against her skin like a musical growl, she whispered, "And it's said that I'm quick to learn."

She inhaled a gasp of surprise when he abruptly left her to pick up the oars and send the punt flying down the river to the dock now in view. Suspecting the reason for his purpose, she scrambled to find, tug on her wet shoes, and tie the laces.

"Joss, why the haste?"

"Look at the trees." He nodded at the trees swaying in the increasing wind. "See how the undersides of the leaves are showing?"

She plopped a hand on top of her hat to hold it on her head. "Yes, silvery."

"It means that shortly it will rain."

"I never noticed that about the leaves looking like that." When the hat's brim began to lift, she double-knotted the ribbons under her chin. Twisting to look over her shoulder, she saw darkening clouds billowing, rolling closer. "And here I thought you wanted to hurry home for instructional purposes."

Grinning and pulling mightily on the oars, he said,

"That, too. Almost there. Get ready to run."

He lashed the boat to the dock and hoisted her up onto the wooden planks. Laughing from nervous excitement, she yanked on his arm to stop him from towing her too quickly across the landing. He stopped when they got on the lawn and away from the water, where he looked down, hair tousled, jacket missing, and shirt undone but smiling hugely.

Long, sinuous willow branches were beginning to whip wildly in the increasing wind as he yelled, "Come along, now. It's time to get busy, my Bea."

Choking to get the words out around the laughter, she crooked a finger to bring his head closer. "Joss, would it be too forward of me if I suggest that we *race* the rest of the way? Winner gets to wear her clothes and watch while he undresses."

Anyone observing his kiss this time—right out in the open for all the world to witness—would witness an indecent display of husbandly ardor. She didn't care and held on for the ride. Then she learned the nicest thing—that it was possible to laugh and run at the same time and that it wasn't important to outrun the rain. Especially when racing home with a man who loved you for all the things you were and never wanted you to change.

Epilogue

Joss sat on a swing with a chubby toddler on his lap. Shifting dots of sunlight came and went through oak leaves overhead, setting aglow his daughter's white-blond hair. A humid summer breeze swept across the lawn, ruffling the riot of curls. Swing ropes creaked as he used boot heels dug into the turf to lazily move him and his gurgling, squirming child. Little Sophie wasn't sleeping well due to the advent of more teeth.

He watched Beatrice, lying on her back on a tartan rug under the oak tree's shade. She was totally immersed in whatever she was reading, as she usually was. She was with child again, which didn't bother her, but did concern him. It turned out that she was rather frighteningly fertile. And interested in making lots of children. She had plans for teaching them. Probably the lofty ideals of Marcus Aurelius before they could walk.

"I say, Bea?"

She hummed a reply, turned a page, and stayed immersed. Before he could get her attention, Sophie got his by sinking her sharp teeth into his chest. When he yelped and tugged free his flesh and shirt, his daughter laughed and waved her arms, grinning up at him.

"Stop that, you fiendish girl." But he gave the reprimand with affection and kissed Sophie's laughing mouth.

Beatrice finally looked up. "Did you say

something?"

"Attempted it. Your child is possessed by deviltry."

Beatrice went back to her book. "No, she's not. She's happy and brilliant. And adores her father."

"She's made my trouser leg damp and her bite nearly pierced my skin right through the material."

Sitting up and using a nearby leaf as a place mark, she closed it and extended her hands. "Give her to me. I'll let her crawl about and pick some grass. I'm sure that's why she's misbehaving. She wants free."

Joss set Sophie down and watched her scuttle across the rug to the grass. She uprooted fistfuls and shoved the green threads poking through her fist into her mouth. He continued to move the swing slowly back and forth, and asked, "Bea, is that wise?"

"Probably not." Hauling Sophie by a foot onto the rug, she inserted a finger and removed the grass. Sophie squawked and started to screw up her face for a tantrum until Bea took a hard ginger biscuit from a pocket and handed it over. His beautiful daughter lunged at it, cramming it into her mouth, and gnawing at it in a most unfeminine manner.

His wife slanted a look up at him to issue a warning. "Don't tell Nursey."

"Since it's keeping her quiet, I don't think I will. How did you do that without losing your finger?"

"Technique. She's always sticking things into her mouth that must be removed. And it worries me that she's always hungry. Did your mother ever mention a predilection for gluttony?"

He eased off the swing and stretched out on the rug beside her. Setting the closed book out of the way, he

176

leaned over to nuzzle her hair. "We were boys. Always hungry. Like me, right now."

Eyes closed, her head moved in languid reply to his. She sleepily murmured, "I thought you wanted to not do this. Abstain or something."

"You're already increasing. Can't be more increasing, can you?"

She withdrew and gazed at him with a contented smile. "How true. And fortuitous. After you deliver our daughter to Nursey, and do get rid of the biscuit before."

"Ordering me about, are you."

"Only suggesting you hurry. I was thinking about that exceptionally tall willow upstream. The one with the lovely hidden alcove underneath? If we're careful, we won't overturn the punt."

"Oh-ho. Now you've given me another i-word for my ritual prayer of gratitude. Tonight I shall add inventive."

"Joss, whatever are you talking about?"

"It's a game I've played since I met you. Adding up a list of adjectives that describe you."

"Such as?"

"Integrity, intelligence, innocence."

"Afraid that's gone by the wayside."

To prove it, she kissed him. That was another blessing that came with an educated wife. She knew how to apply instruction and he'd given her a great deal of his own kind of education since the night long ago when he'd made a hash of it.

As he scooped up Sophie, Beatrice rolled onto her not yet round tummy and waved her sandal-clad feet in the air. With an impish grin, she added, "Don't forget ingenious, and I'm getting *impatient*."

"Insatiable, too. You are the perfect wife, Lady Warfield."

"At the quick march, Sir Jocelyn."

And he obeyed.

Dear Reader, If you enjoyed, *To Jilt a Corinthian,* please consider writing a review. An excerpt from the next book in this series, *More Than a Milkmaid,* and *Avenue to Heaven,* a western historical, follow this list of titles also written by Julia Donner, aka M.L. Rigdon.

Thanks for your friendship and continued support! Here is the link to join me on BookBub: https://www.bookbub.com/authors/julia-donner

Julia/Mary Lou

Writing Historical Fiction as Julia Donner
The Friendship series

THE TIGRESSE AND THE RAVEN
THE HEIRESS AND THE SPY
THE RAKE AND THE BISHOP'S DAUGHTER
THE DUCHESS AND THE DUELIST
THE EARL AND THE RUNAWAY
THE DANDY AND THE FLIRT
LORD CARNALL AND MISS INNOCENT
THE BARBARIAN AND HIS LADY
A ROGUE FOR MISS PRIM
AN AMERICAN FOR AGNES
A LAIRD'S PROMISE
TO JILT A CORINTHIAN
MORE THAN A MILKMAID (2019)

Westward Bound Series

AVENUE TO HEAVEN
NO EASY STREET (Winter 2018)
DROVER'S LANE (2019)

Writing as M.L.Rigdon

Fantasy
Seasons of Time **trilogy**
PROPHECY DENIED
BEYOND THE DARK MOUNTAINS
HER QUEST FOR THE LANCE

Contemporary
THE ATLANTIS CRYSTAL (A Philadelphia Hafeldt novel)
SEDUCTIVE MINES (Another Phil Hafeldt adventure)
NEVER LET ME DIE (Romantic suspense)

YA Fantasy

Songs of Atlantis **series**
THE VITAL
MASTER OF THE DARK
CANTICLE OF DESTRUCTION
DRAGONAIR (2019)

More Than a Milkmaid (Excerpt)

Friendship Series Book 13

Chapter 1

    Lightning crackled overhead, rattling the cowshed. Lenora placed a calming hand on the Jersey's neck, soothing her with slow strokes. Usually docile and calm, Lord Darcourt's prized dairy cow shifted, her large brown eyes reflecting worry.

Lenora crooned to the Jersey, "All is well, my lovely. Tis only the weather acting up."

The other mixed-bred cows, restless from the electrical storm, might not allow her to milk them. If only it would rain to break the arid tension of the last week.

A fierce gust of wind tore at the roof. One of the cows bawled. She went to stand in the shed's open doors, looking out at treetops swaying in the wind. Sheep huddled in nervous clumps in the pasture below. Still no rain but the atmosphere felt dense with portent. One could only pray that the volatile weather would move on its way if it had no plans to release the tension with a downpour. Minutes later, it did, and she milked what could be had from petulant cows. By the time she finished milking the small herd, the weather had moved off, but the sense of advent, of something coming, persisted.

Then came the chore of carrying buckets to and from the house. Grooms usually helped but were busy receiving the equipages of visitors to Lowbridge Hall. Lord and Lady Darcourt were entertaining, celebrating their fifth year of marriage. It was a happy time, the sort Lenora had dreamed of for herself before unfortunate circumstances changed her life path. She wouldn't dwell on that. All the riches in the world could never replace her Amelia, who turned nine last week and was now safely at home with Aunt Meredith. Four years ago, her sister Hermione joined them at her aunt's snug cottage on Darcourt land.

After lugging milk buckets to the kitchen, Lenora

trudged back to the shed and let the cows out to pasture. The sky remained overcast but clearing, the sun hazy above the treetops. She was grateful not to have to plod home through the woodland in filthy weather to her aunt's cottage on the other side of the copse. The walk was pleasant when it wasn't raining, snowing or sleeting. Making the trek twice a day for the milking wasn't a bother unless the weather turned windy and wet. One early morning she'd nearly been crushed by the sudden fall of a rotted tree limb. She hadn't complained, but Lord Darcourt somehow heard of the incident and had the copse cleared of deadwood.

As she crossed the stable yard, she heard the rattle of an oncoming carriage and stepped out of the way of a phaeton rolling toward the carriage house. Men's voices, orders, banter, and laughter came from within the stable. She accepted an internal call to enter. Watching the tasks of horse and carriage care always soothed; no matter how chaotic, and she didn't know why. Perhaps it reminded her of childhood days, happier times of long pony rides.

Staying well out of the way of the activity in the stable's center aisle, she nodded and smiled at men who waved and called out greetings. There were many faces she didn't recognize, the servants of visiting gentry and aristocrats. She slipped into an open stall and peered out into the wide corridor. The scent of fresh fodder underfoot and hay in the rack soothed the empty feeling of nostalgia and loss.

A groom broke into memories when he handed her a lead line, putting her to work she loved. She pulled the horse inside the roomy stall then cross-tied the gelding. This was not a driving animal or part of a

182

flashy team. The dark chestnut had the sloping lines and longer legs of a hunter, the sort of well set-up horse that cost a fortune and one that she would have had for her own, if her life had turned out differently.

She put those thoughts behind her. That world, those dreams, had moved beyond her reach, but it didn't stop her from the joy of settling the gelding. She rubbed the peak above the withers where the mane ended. She'd seen horses in pasture gnaw at each other there in friendship. When she dug her nails in and scratched, the gelding nodded his head with pleasure and turned his nose toward her when she stopped. Holding his head still, she pressed her face against the velvety muzzle. After they exchanged breaths, she moved along his flank to drape an arm over his rump and watch the activity outside the stall. The gelding cocked a back hoof on its tip and heaved a sigh, contented now to ignore the bustle inside the stable block.

The same groom called as he strode by with a prancing bay, "Got that big fellow calmed down, have ye, Miss Lenora?"

"Already asleep, Jim Wielder."

As the mare moved past, the angry twitch of her long black tail swished into the stall, stinging the back of Lenora's hand. She started to laugh then felt her facial muscles droop at what stood on the other side of the aisle. The mare's body had blocked the view.

Nine hundred years ago, the sight would have sent her fleeing for her life. No helmet covered the back of his head of wavy blond hair. Boots added height he didn't need, already standing a full head above the tallest man in the stable. Shoulders encased in excellently tailored blue superfine looked broader than John Cooper's, the local farrier and fighting champ. This Norseman's build gave the impression of the marauding Viking horde, but his clothes and the way he wore them placed him above the servant class.

Another team of horses blocked him from sight, and she reached out and grabbed Jim Wielder's arm as he walked by to fetch another horse.

She tugged the head groom into the stall. Young for his position, Jim's father and the one before him had worked for the Darcourts. Always neat in his habits and full of good cheer, Jim had made it clear from her first day at Lowbridge Hall that he favored her. He didn't mind that she was a Long Meg who could look him in the eye. Nor was he put off when she kindly turned away his tentative advances. Every spring, he tried another proposal. She'd begun to think it was all in fun but was never quite sure.

"Jim, who is that man?"

He craned his neck to look around. "Which one?"

"The one across the way," she whispered, gesturing with her head.

When another team passed by, the Norseman was gone, now striding toward the stable entrance. Jim looked in the direction of her point.

"Oh. That's Jack. Jack Cervantes, Sir Jocelyn's valet. Guess they'll be calling him Warfield up at the house."

She peeked around the end of the stall. "He looks more like a lord than a valet."

"Some of them gentlemen's gentlemen do, you know. Look at you. You sound like you should be up at the house, dishing up tea and tasties."

184

She huffed a derisive laugh. "Those days are long gone, Jim."

"He's on his way back. Now, you best be a good girl and behave. No flirting, Miss Lenora."

She swatted his arm for teasing then abruptly halted when the Norseman stopped to look at her. A vague familiarity about his blue-eyed stare made her heart slow to sluggish thumps. It couldn't be. He'd died ten, horribly long years ago. And yet, there was something about the valet's gaze, especially when disinterest became something else, brightening with a spark of recognition then stunned comprehension.

She fled, moving as swiftly as possible without disturbing the horses. The feeling of being chased made the flesh on her back cringe. Pressure spread throughout her chest. Wild emotion clogged her throat, inciting the acute urge to weep.

A man's voice behind her called, "Lenora!"

No, it couldn't be. It wasn't possible. Swelling tears that blurred her vision spilled, scorching her cheeks. She hurried faster, now desperate to flee, but he called again, "Nora, wait!"

That familiar but different voice didn't stop her, but the name he called out brought her to a halt. No one but Philippe called her Nora. No one had since the day he died, when no one spoke his name again. Her dreams were buried with him, and with the name that was never again spoken, only etched on a headstone.

She slowly turned around. Ten years ago, he'd been slender, too tall and angular, his white-blond curls always in disarray, his expression always mischievous and cheerful. The years had darkened his complexion and hair. Maturity had broadened his frame, but the sky-blue eyes were the same. Except now, the merry glint was absent.

Anger, fear, despair clogged her brain when he stopped few steps away. He looked larger than her Philippe, too different. This wasn't the lad who'd broken her heart, ruined her reputation, destroyed their future. Emotions too devastating to confront choked off her panting breaths until she could do nothing but glare her pain and resentment.

All she could think of to say was, "You're dead."

Chapter 2

He didn't know which hurt more, her wide-eyed fear when she recognized him or the growing hostility in the eyes of the one person he loved more than life itself. For a moment he'd gone dizzy from the unexpectedness of her seeing in the stable, the impossibility of it.

She'd altered a great deal from fragile, shy girl to woman. The silky-fine, light brown hair she'd always worn down and held back with a ribbon was now hidden under a plain mobcap. Why did she have on barn clogs and a soiled apron over a peasant frock?

Confusion swamped him again. Memories of her had haunted him for a decade. His Nora lived in his memory as either a comfort or a misery, but always as the sweet-natured girl his family had chosen for him to marry. And now she was dressed like a servant? His mind refused to absorb Miss Lenora Jane Asher of Underhill Manor as a member of the working class. More shocking than all else was the enmity, the outright hatred in her eyes.

"Nora, what are you doing here? Why are you dressed like that?"

She took a step back. "It should be obvious. I'm a dairymaid. Why are you alive?"

He started to ask for a better explanation but felt curious eyes watching. One of the stable lads was giving him an intense visual warning. Bloody hell, she

187

hadn't sunk to marrying a servant, had she?

Eager to touch her, to confirm that this moment was real and that he wasn't dreaming, he took her arm. "Come, let's move away from the stable. Go somewhere quieter to talk."

She jerked her arm free, cheeks flaming, and said in a furious whisper, "I can't be seen talking to you. I'll lose my position."

Her forearm felt different, astonishingly firm, muscular. The discovery intensified his bewilderment. He struggled to remember what was said last then tried a stupid tack, a feeble attempt to placate. "Lady Darcourt is too kind-hearted for that."

"She is, but her housekeeper is not. Now that Lady Warfield is no longer around to lend Lady Darcourt a backbone, it's off I'll be sent, and without a reference."

"Lady Warfield has returned for the celebration. She's up at the house with Sir Jocelyn. What are you doing here at Lowbridge? Why you working?"

"One tends not to survive very long without food." She marched toward the house, adding over her shoulder as he hurried to follow, "And Father's widow turned us off."

"Us? You married a servant?"

She lowered her voice to a hiss as a housemaid walked by them, giving them an odd look. "Don't be dense. My sister."

Relief that she hadn't married a servant or anyone else, got tangled with the bewilderment of her present situation. "Hermione came with you? She is just a girl."

"She's eighteen, Phil—"

He interrupted her by taking her arm and pulling her with him around the corner of the house, out of
188

sight of the stable. He pressed her into the foliage of the wisteria that covered the back wall. "Don't call me that. I'm Cervantes now. Or Jack."

"You are no one to me, sir, a stranger."

She used a sleeve to dash away tears slipping from brown eyes that had been sweet and adoring in his memory, not flashing with defiance, like now. His mind went blank again. Then their last time together burst to life—his begging her forgiveness. Her eyes had filled with tears, exactly as they were now, but beseeching, begging to go with him. Today she blazed with angry passion, nothing like the placid girl and the life he'd been forced to abandon.

He glanced around for a more private place to talk, but there was activity everywhere. Keeping an eye on the servants' entrance, he asked, "Nora, what happened? All this time...I expected you'd married, have a brood of children by now. You look so...altered."

In a low, mutinous voice she accused, "Neither are you the same. You're a servant like myself. And you kept growing."

He hadn't realized that he'd been holding her by the shoulders, pinning her against the wisteria-covered back of the house, until her work-roughened fingers pried at his grip. Something desperate that he'd buried deep inside refused to let her escape.

Impatient and tense, she said, "We can't be seen like this, and you must get away from here. Brissard is one of the guests."

Sudden worry tightened his grasp on her. "What is Uncle George doing here?"

"Not him. Your cousin Henry."

A chill crawled over his flesh. Not thinking, he jerked Nora into his arms. Every nerve crackled to life. Henry, the one person who could bring all of his plans, everything he'd worked so hard and long to accomplish to nothing. A word from his cousin and all would be lost. He had no guarantee that Henry would keep his promise.

A rush of fear had him protectively shielding as much of Nora as he could with arms and body when a sudden presence and authoritative voice snapped, "Cervantes, what in blazes are you about? Let go of that girl."

Inhaling a deep breath, he released Nora, who stood with head bowed. When a lad, he'd been charmed by her shyness. Now, her submissive posture sparked outrage. She had nothing to be ashamed of if she'd been forced to take employment.

"Joss, she's known to me."

"I can see that much, but I've never known you to take advantage of the servants."

"Blast it all, Joss, climb down from that high horse. Nora, this is Sir Jocelyn Warfield. Sir Jocelyn, Miss Lenora Jane Asher of Underhill Manor."

His friend and employer's attitude instantly changed. Surprise briefly flickered over his face then remolded back to aloof disinterest. Joss removed a monocle and nodded a grave, polite bow. A silent question drew his black eyebrows into a startled scowl when Nora reacted. Years of formal indoctrination straightened her spine from the humble servant pose. She dipped a slow, shallow curtsy, head tilted slightly, the graceful, polite greeting drilled into every girl of good family. There was no mistaking that automatic
190

response, different in every way from a servant's. She ruined it with a flustered blush, realizing her error too late.

It didn't seem possible, but Joss found a higher horse to climb on when he said, "How very pleased I am to meet you, Miss Asher. Do forgive the intrusion, but I must beg leave to speak with my manservant without delay."

Before he could stop her, Nora whirled and fled into the back of the house. Joss grabbed his arm when he started to follow.

"Let go of me, Joss."

"No, Jack, confound it. Leave the girl be. We have a more important issue that's come up."

"I don't care."

When he started to go after Nora, Joss stepped in front of him, blocking the way. "You had better. I've just got done talking with Brissard." Joss paused to examine the reaction to that news. "I thought that would put a spoke in your wheel."

"Henry knows I'm here?"

Joss sneered and added a snort of contempt. "It is a wonder to me how the two of you can share common blood. The fool tried to condescend to my Bea."

"I have no doubt that she twisted him into a few knots. So, he doesn't know that I'm here?"

"No, but besides myself and the young lady who just left, he's the only other person who knows who you really are and that you're alive. And before you ask, my wife doesn't know. Even if she did, my Bea would never divulge. The rack couldn't get a secret out of her. No smirking, if you please. You are never on the receiving end of her clever intent. It scares me down right down to the ground, and if my good eye hasn't yet failed me, Miss Asher does the same to you."

"She does. Always has. We were contracted quite young. I grew up thinking nothing else but that we would one day wed."

Joss murmured as a footman loaded with luggage swiftly walked by. "And tragedy struck. What is she doing here, acting like a servant?"

"I have no idea, but I will definitely find out."

AVENUE TO HEAVEN (available now)

Chicago, Illinois

August, 1891

Chapter 1

The coffin had been delivered to her doorstep sometime during the night. Annie stared down at the crudely cut box. The remaining servants had found it under the portico at dawn and pushed it through the front door, hopefully before the neighbors had seen it.

After sending the servants away, she inhaled a fortifying breath in preparation for examining the thing, a calling card from her former husband. Life had become a game of avoiding the past, a constant struggle while surrounded by reminders. It meant residing in this house where the ugliness had occurred, finding the courage to confront the message inside the coffin.

One of the servants had set a crowbar on top of the coarse, wood planks. The black metal felt cold and awkwardly heavy. The screech of protesting nails echoed off the hammered-tin ceiling. The lifted lid exposed a life-size, wax rendition of herself as she'd looked a decade ago.

She tilted her head sideways to assess it. There were more dreadful things in life than a naked, wax duplication of oneself, such as living with the sender. Any attempt to misconstrue the delivery as a sentimental token was ruined by the addition of a knife buried in the glossy chest. After smothering a startled choke, she regained outward poise and quickly replaced the packing straw over the lurid figurine. She shoved the coffin lid shut, ignoring the macabre squeal of nails scraping against unseasoned wood. She picked up the crowbar to drive nails back into place.

Through clenched teeth she muttered with each strike, "A rather pointed declaration of intent, Charles."

She forgave herself for the maudlin pun. It hadn't been so easy to forgive herself for marrying Charles Corday. She'd been little more than a child when she had, if not in years, certainly in maturity. Most of her illusions had been shattered during the six, nightmarish years of marriage to him. Hardened from those years, she'd reacted with only a moment of shock over the coffin's contents.

The crowbar made a hollow thump when she set it on the lid. It was rather too bad that the figurine had to be destroyed. Her parsimonious nature debated the waste. The artist was actually quite good, except for the face. There was something empty and yet sinister about the fixed smile. The rest of the wax model was perfection, right down to the delicate blue veins and pale rose and cream hues of her bosom. Her replica wore nothing but the packing straw—added shock value, of course—so there could be no doubt that this threat had come from someone who knew her intimately. Since there was no one around, she gave the box a spiteful kick.

It didn't help. A chill slithered over her arms and shoulders. Charles was coming back to Chicago and this hideous joke, his declaration. She thought she'd prepared herself for his return, but even the most meticulous of preparations can neither duplicate nor prepare one for reality.

She went to the bell pull and yanked. Moments later, a young, freckled housemaid flounced into the parlor. "An' what would you be needin', Mrs. Corday?"

Annie hid the knife she'd withdrawn in the folds of her skirt and attempted to casually ask, "Have Sven and Henry left for the Schneider's?"

"Not 'til that barn's been cleaned out, if they know what's good for 'em. They've taken the horses to auction."

"Bridie, when they return, would you please have the men carry this box into the butler's pantry? Chop up the wax inside. Render it down and pour it into buckets. Have the wax delivered to Hull House."

"Yes, ma'am."

"And Bridie, I would consider it a great favor if you would see to this task by yourself. Except for the hauling of it. When you open the lid, you will know why the men must not see what is inside. I shall be resting in my room until Mrs. Barnes arrives."

Upstairs in her bedroom, a refreshing breeze lifted window curtains. Even though she'd slept very little the night before, plagued by the usual dreams, sleep continued to elude. There was too much to think about, too much to do. She eventually got up and went to the tall window. Using a finger to draw aside the curtain's

195

filmy lace, she peeked around its edge to study the Gothic Revival residence on the other side of Clark Street. A stout matron tromped down the shallow steps under its portico.

Mrs. Hiller made no physical excuses about being a female determined to halt the process of time by exerting ruthless control over her face and figure. She'd been crammed into a frilly yellow-and-red-striped carriage ensemble and carried a yapping ball of fluff under one arm. With her other hand, she gestured rude instructions with a bilious green parasol.

Annie murmured with a smirk, "I wager they had to lace you up tighter than a pickle barrel to get you into that."

She huffed a cynical snort. Such was the incredible hodgepodge of Chicago, where the hoi polloi rubbed elbows with the city's *haute ton* of the self-made. She didn't disdain the crass behaviors of the newly rich. She'd come down so far in the world that she couldn't afford to cast any social stones. She was as intrigued with neighbors she never consorted with as they were fascinated with Mrs. Annamarie Lawrence Corday, formerly married to one of the most terrifying men to ever crawl up from Chicago's dangerous underworld.

Grinning at the commotion across the street, Annie whispered in a grinning rendition of Bridie's brogue, "And what sort of a mischief is herself up to at this time of a mornin'?"

Mrs. Hiller aimed her instructions at a stoic, liveried driver of the landau waiting at the base of the portico steps. An elegant team of bob-tailed chestnuts with gloriously white stockings stood patiently alert— as utterly well-bred as Mrs. Hiller was not. Two footmen hoisted Mrs. Hiller into the open carriage, careful to avoid her yappy pet. After settling the dog, Mrs. Hiller swiveled sideways on the velvet-tufted seat. She raised a lorgnette and aimed it at the Corday Greek Revival, totally unaware she was being studied in turn.

Annie chuckled. "Can't see me, can you, old girl?"

Mrs. Hiller and everyone else in town were frantic for news. The latest gossip burning across the city featured the rumor of Charles Corday's return. All of Chicago waited, some merely curious, but many eager for the flash of dirty linen. More than a few hastily packed to get out of town before Corday found them.

She'd let the curious know what she needed them to know, when she wanted them to know it. She'd learned to painstakingly plot every aspect of her life, even the pruning of the immense elm tree outside her bedroom window. The limbs had been shaped for seeing out, while preventing the inquisitive from seeing inside.

She allowed the curtain to fall back into place and went down the curved staircase to wait for her friend. How she would miss Charlotte's friendship, but sacrifices had to be made when it came to outwitting evil. Her survival plan was a startling one, to be sure— unconventional and certainly convoluted—but crucial for survival in a world where Charles existed and wanted her dead.

Chapter 2

Having given up on a nap, she went downstairs to wait for Charlotte. Crossing the foyer, she noticed the quiet. The house stood eerily silent now that most of the servants had been sent to other positions. It felt odd, the stillness. Almost loud.

Vibrant sunlight slanted through tall parlor windows. The elongated reception room had been strategically cluttered with Belter furniture and thriving potted plants. Plush velvet draperies were heavy enough to hide behind or shut out the world.

She went directly to the bay window, avoiding the presence of the sheet-draped coffin and the immense portrait on the wall. The padded window seat was her favorite place to soak up sunlight. After Charles fled, she redecorated the parlor but hadn't taken down her portrait. An inner voice whispered it must be kept as a reminder of how she must always be strong and vigilant. She must never again be weak or undecided. That was the past. The circumstance of life had to be controlled to create a future full of new possibilities. But only if she could outwit Charles again, stay a step ahead.

The sunshine felt as soothing as she imagined a lover's caress might be. The warmth helped to melt the fear lodged in her chest. She did nap, propped up with a pillow behind her back and one on her lap, until Charlotte arrived.

"Annamarie, my dear, why are you asleep? We had a date."

Annie blinked away sun and sleep. She smiled at

her friend. Chicago's most beautiful matron, Charlotte Barnes, with her moonlight pale hair, cupid's bow mouth and elegant wasp waist stood in the parlor doorway. Charlotte's much vaunted countenance sported a frown.

"Annamarie, is it indeed true? That dreadful beast is coming back?"

Covering a yawn with the backs of her fingers, Annie stood. "His calling card arrived this morning."

Charlotte pressed a lacy handkerchief to her cheek. "Oh, my dearest, whatever shall you do?"

"I shall ring for Bridie and have her bring us tea. Or would you prefer a cool drink? Do sit down, Charlotte."

"How can you talk of tea at a time like this?" Charlotte wilted gracefully onto a satin-sheathed sofa.

Annie pinched back a grin. Charlotte, the epitome of womanliness, had a backbone of tempered steel. She positioned her glorious figure, while scattering reticule, parasol, and gloves. An Impressionist couldn't have arranged a more suitable pose.

The skirt of Charlotte's morning ensemble fell in shining folds of mauve *crepe de Chine* under a matching jacket. The broad, round wheel of her hat slanted on mounds of pale hair, the whole covered with a frothy film of mauve and pink netting. She'd anchored this glorious confection in place with amethyst-tipped hatpins. A corsage of pink roses had been pinned to the jacket's left shoulder, placed there to match the double row of silk-covered buttons that marched down the jacket's front, which had been gored to fit like a second skin.

In the suffocating humidity of Chicago in August,

Charlotte presented the perfect image of cool, fashionable femininity. Feeling entirely unequal to her friend's poised splendor, Annie hid her nerves by strolling around the room to check the soil in the scattered flowerpots with fear-chilled fingertips.

Charlotte's tone was devoid of its usual airy quality when she repeated, "What will you do, Annamarie? He has killed off all the witnesses."

"Do? Why, I suppose I shall have to remarry."

An awkward silence followed. Annie needed to avoid her friend's clever eyes while she explained her dangerous and more than a little outrageous plan. Although her friend portrayed the perfect rendition of vacant feminine charm, Charlotte was as shrewd and focused as any politician on the scent of a juicy bribe.

If she could get her friend's acceptance and assistance, her plan might work. She needed someone in Chicago to send her reports of Charles, someone he wouldn't dare harm.

"Charlotte, have you ever heard of ordering a bride by mail?"

Charlotte's reply oozed disdain. "Good heavens, please assure me that you're not thinking of responding to an unsavory advertisement."

"Certainly not. I am the one shopping for a spouse."

She peered out of the corner of her eye to assess Charlotte's reaction and discovered her friend too shocked to let fly with another question.

"Well, I don't see why I should not. Why can't I get myself a convenient spouse? Men do it all the time. No one questions them. There should be nothing wrong with a lady doing the same."

Charlotte discarded the veil of simpleminded helplessness. "You cannot be serious. Women do not *advertise* for a spouse. It's pitiful enough that a female should find herself reduced to answering such an embarrassing public notice, but a female actively recruiting for a husband is unconscionable!"

"Oh, for goodness sake, Charlotte. Women spend the better part of their lives in subtle pursuit of men, and I most certainly have *not* placed an advertisement. My perspective husband and bodyguard is someone Harold knows, a Mr. Jacob Williams of Prosperous, Colorado."

"Harold? *Harold Browne*? You can't reply on him! All that groveling and obnoxious adoration of you is beyond all bounds."

Feeling a bit stung, she coolly replied, "Perhaps I am not insulted by his admiration, Charlotte. I am not a reigning beauty with the entire male population of Chicago at my feet."

Charlotte looked away with a delicate sniff. "What nonsense. You know my aim is to promote James in any manner I can. Short of adultery. He'll make a fine mayor one day."

"Yes, Charlotte, he will. He is one of the few who do not fear Charles."

"I still insist that you reconsider this plan. There is no comparison between my willingness to see my husband safely installed in the mayoral office and the sort of intrigues hatched in Harold Browne's twisted brain."

"Harold has never failed me. He invested the little cash Charles left behind, and in doing so, has made me a great deal of money. By acting as my agent, none of my fellow investors ever knew that they had a female as a controlling partner."

Charlotte looked away. "I find that suspect in itself. That man is altogether too clever and slippery. I don't care if the little weasel is in love with you. I've never trusted him and neither does James."

"Then what would you have me do? Shall I sit here and wait for Charles to have his revenge on me? Perhaps I should run for the rest of my life, wondering if he is behind the door, or lurking around the next corner. I tell you, Charlotte, I *will* have a life for myself. I got rid of him once before, and I shall do so again!"

Charlotte raised blond eyebrows. "Am I expected to condone this sort of rash venture without offering the tiniest objection or merest suggestion of advice? You're my dearest friend, Annamarie. I cannot and will not stand quietly by while you ruin your life a second time."

"Ruination or not, I intend to stay alive and in one piece. And if all goes well, I shall be free of him forever."

Charlotte's eyes narrowed. Her cupid's bow lips thinned into a line. Before she could say another protest, Annie took Charlotte's hand and drew her to the sheet-draped coffin. The nails didn't squeak as loudly this time, but the impact of the contents remained as visceral.

Annie said, "Regard the hole in the chest. It is where I removed a knife."

Lips parted, her face frozen in surprise, Charlotte wordlessly stared. After few moments, she murmured, "You had best tell me how I might help.

202

Chapter 3

The following day, Annie examined herself in front of a full-length mirror. Harold had suggested she alter her appearance to discourage any unwanted attentions from Mr. Williams. After assessing her reflection in the carved rosewood mirror, she was glad she'd sent Perkins to her new situation as Charlotte's dresser. A glance at this and poor Mrs. Perkins would suffer an apoplexy.

Twisting to peer over her shoulder, she marveled at the graceless drape of cheap, brown cotton. The cord trimming of puce and mustard rendered the readymade skirt comical. She had to hide her bosom somehow, and the too large shirtwaist gave her upper-half a lumpy rather than curvaceous appearance. She gnawed her upper lip. Perhaps the off-putting ensemble might be a bit too obvious. She was a wealthy woman, after all. To appear entirely unfashionable might invite suspicion.

Her shoulders drooped as she stared. Her waist had expanded to an unsightly eighteen inches without a corset. Damaged ribs refused to allow for even the slightest cinching of her waist. Due to the first beating from Charles, tight lacing of any kind created slicing pains in her ribs with every breath.

Charlotte often slept in her corset to achieve her fifteen inches. Now that her friend was with child, she would never reach her goal of a fourteen-inch wasp waist, which was probably for the better. Charlotte neglected a fine mind due to her preoccupation with vanity.

She huffed a sigh at her own shortcomings and reached for a silver-backed hand mirror. The puffy pompadour was presently the mode, or the precisely arranged curls she preferred. This morning, she twined her hair into a black braid then pinned it into a painfully tight spiral at the back of her head. No ribbons, flowers, or decorative pins relieved the cruel arrangement.

She wrinkled her nose at the result. "*Horrifique.*"

Setting aside the mirror, she reached for the final touch, spectacles with tinted lenses. She perched the glasses on the bridge of her nose and wrapped the thin wires around her ears. The round lenses enhanced her owlish expression. Quivering lips and a snort of laughter ruined the stern image.

The distant thump of the doorknocker echoed up the staircase. With a startled gasp, she realized that Harold Browne was late. What if it wasn't Harold and she had to deal with Mr. Williams alone?

Her old ankle injury complained as she hurried down the steps and across the foyer. Harold flew through the door she held open and went directly to the marble-topped table by the entry to set down his bowler.

He fussed with an armload of papers as he scolded, "You shouldn't be opening the door, Mrs. Corday. Where are the servants? What if it had been Charles and not I at the door?"

"I sent them to their new situations yesterday. Bridie has gone next door to deliver a package."

"My dear lady, you can't be thinking of staying in this huge house all alone."

He didn't give her an opportunity to answer. He stopped fiddling with the papers and fully focused on her for the first time. She enjoyed an oddly ironical reaction of gratification from his gaping expression.

204

Scandalized, he whispered, "Mrs. Corday, what have you *done* to yourself?"

"Only what you suggested, Mr. Browne. I have minimized my charms."

She turned and walked with brisk purpose across the white marble that paved the vestibule. A long carpet runner led to the office at the end of the corridor. Its softness helped with the little pinches of pain stabbing her left ankle with every step. She shouldn't have run from the south wing and down the steps. After this interview, she'd have the remainder of the day to rest and elevate her storm-predicting ankle. It always acted up before a weather change or after hard usage.

As Harold entered the office behind her, she instructed, "Please allow the door to stand partially open. I think you should occupy the desk, since you will be conducting the interview. I shall take this chair, which will present an unobstructed view of Mr. Williams while you negotiate."

"Certainly, Mrs., Corday!"

"You shall direct him to sit there." She gestured to a lattice-backed chair in front of the sprawling mahogany desk. She'd selected the chair because it had a sturdy military appearance suitable for the occasion.

"Just as you wish," Harold chirped while arranging papers.

Annie sat and folded her hands in her lap. "You were tardy, Mr. Browne. I hope you did not sustain a distressing accident."

"Not at all. Merely a bit of unpleasantness with the casino proprietor. But all is well. There's nothing quite like the results produced from the efficacy of large sums of currency."

Her heart began to race. "He will cause no trouble?"

Harold replied with a smirk. "I've taken precautions to insure that everyone complies. And I really must compliment you, Mrs. Corday. You don't look at all like yourself. A womanizer like my brother will be *utterly* discouraged."

She took a moment to digest that convoluted accolade. "Thank you, Mr. Browne. I must admit to a measure of concern, if not confusion. You assured me that your brother is more than capable of protecting me from Charles and also expressed your belief that he will honor all aspects of the agreement. I do not find myself as entirely confident as to his trustworthiness as you, no matter how well you have manipulated the individuals involved."

He smiled and cleared his throat. "Perhaps I should've mentioned that he's only my *half*-brother. His character is not as socially developed as my own. His father was a…deviant sort."

"You are absolutely certain he can protect me from a man like Clovis."

She didn't care for the hint of condescension when Harold replied, "Nothing to worry about there. Even the worst of Corday's henchmen shouldn't be of concern. Part of my brother's dilemma with the casino is that he did a great deal of damage structurally to the casino itself and physically to its ruffians. Numerous bones were broken and one of the casino roughnecks has yet to regain consciousness."

"What caused this commotion? Unwillingness to pay a gambling debt?"

Harold aligned the document corners with the

papers underneath. "I believe a *female* was involved."

She blinked to dispel uneasiness. "I am not sufficiently reassured, neither for my own safety or that he will agree to this plan."

"He won't back out, Mrs. Corday. He has no other choice."

"Sir, you have also made obvious your distaste for your own sibling. You imply he possesses habits inconsistent with that which we would like to behold in a gentleman. To be perfectly candid, Mr. Browne, will my person be safe in his company?"

Harold sneered and she couldn't help but remember when Charlotte likened him to a greasy toad. "Ma'am, you are a lady of refinement, impeccable lineage, and superior understanding. Ergo, my brother and you have nothing whatsoever in common. You might take into consideration his choice of lodging. A brothel, no matter how high-toned, should be a clear indication of his preferences. You are decidedly not the sort of female he wishes to…entertain."

This wasn't reassuring. She'd enough experience with the opposite sex to know that even the most sensitive weren't to be trusted. A woman's education or inbred refinement had little influence, if any, with the intentions of an avidly aroused male. Men weren't attracted to what was between a woman's ears. Their main goal was located farther south. Good manners restricted voicing this opinion or other such delicate concerns with a member of the opposite gender.

Unable to suppress curiosity, she asked, "Where is he staying?"

Contempt twisted his thin, dry lips. "He's spent his entire time in Chicago at Haven House. I was told that

207

the exorbitant membership fees were waived for reasons not explained."

Haven House was one of Chicago's most elite bordellos. Her hands fisted from the sudden memory of noisy, garishly painted women—the prostitutes Charles kept in residence for his cronies. Their high-pitched, brittle laughter and harsher personalities had left an indelible impression, especially the vicious, big blond Clovis favored. The vulgar commotion she and Clovis made every night had been so loud that their coupling echoed throughout the mansion. Charles had found the pair amusing, until the blond made the mistake of annoying him.

The crackle of shuffling papers brought her back to the present, returning her to the unsettling image she'd begun to create, as Harold muttered, "Where is the lout?"

After readjusting the spectacles on his beaked nose, he tugged at the constriction of his celluloid shirt collar. She looked away from the clenching and unclenching of his thin fingers. There was something strident and unbalanced about his behavior, something vengeful. She had the uncomfortable suspicion he was looking forward to this interview with his brother for very unpleasant reasons. She flinched when the doorknocker sounded.

Chapter 4

Before she could rise up to answer, the patter of Bridie's slippers flew past the office door left ajar. Muffled voices drifted down the corridor, one lilting and laughing, the other deep and muted.

208

Beads of moisture dotted Harold's wide, pale brow that he hastily blotted with a handkerchief. He shoved the rumpled linen into a pocket as footsteps approached.

Bridie's frizzy, orange-haired head peered around the door's edge. "There's a Mr. Williams callin'. He doesn't have a card. Should I bring him through?"

A nod sent Bridie flying up the hallway as Harold muttered, "He should've used the servants' entrance."

She hushed him and strained to hear Bridie's excited chatter. Her giggles and musical laughter was followed by a muffled masculine remark.

Just outside the door, Bridie cooed an answer, "Oh, sir, ain't you the clever one, callin' this place a mausoleum. Why, Mrs. Hiller's filthy pile across the street is more like. Here's the office."

The door eased open wider, exposing Bridie in profile as she held the white china doorknob. She stared up in girlish awe and squirming delight. The caller stood behind the partially opened door. Only his hand showed, tanned and knuckles scraped. The hat he held was straight-brimmed and low-crowned, an unconventional style in comparison to the bowler currently in fashion. It reminded her of what a caballero would wear. She'd expected a Stetson, the headwear of choice of all the visiting cattle barons.

A great deal could be surmised from a man's hat and shoes. This man's hat, although not in fashion, was expensive, not readymade or off the shelf. The tips of his boots gleamed with a recent shine, the kind that can only be achieved from the best leather. Was the famous abbess of Haven House buying his clothes?

She pressed her spine against the back of the chair

from an unsettling feeling, a premonition, the hint of something indefinable, yet darkly inviting. A chill sped up her arms and invaded her scalp under the tightly pinned braid. She'd learned to never ignore her instincts and studied the uncomfortable reaction—one that warned her this man could be dangerous.

She abruptly looked at Harold, who had an unobstructed view of his brother. Her usually bland and obsequious financial advisor now wore an expression of profound loathing and gleeful hatred.

Sudden doubts flooded her mind about this scheme for a temporary husband and protector. Her fears were swept aside by the caller's husky, laughing response to Bridie's attempts to flirt with a man most likely old enough to have fathered her. What had gotten into the girl?

"Oh, sir, won't you let me take your hat? Would you like me to brush it for you?"

Her empty stomach roiled. She pushed down an almost ungovernable urge to jump up and slap the girl, which was completely stilled when Williams spoke.

"I'd be right obliged if you'd take it, Miss Bridie, but there's no call for you to do any extra work."

His voice was sand and softness, like liquid heat caressing the air. A shaft of impatience, at herself for feeling thrilled, and at Bridie for making a vulgar display, brought her back to task.

Bridie squirmed in place, staring up in awe as she offered, "Oh, no, Mr. Williams. T'will be no work at all. I'll give it a nice brush off and set it on the table in the vestibule. You know where I mean? By the front door?"

A smile could be heard in his reply. "Thank you,

miss."

She clamped down on her molars to suppress the urge to give Bridie a reprimand. Aggravation evaporated when the caller stepped through the doorway. Every muscle in her body clenched.

Jacob Williams didn't resemble his brother in any way. Where Harold was frail and nondescript, his brother was much taller and possessed a vibrant presence. An aura of virility and restrained power entered with him. It was no wonder Bridie had been rendered stupid, but when Williams turned his gaze on her, she realized he was furious. She didn't know how she knew this. It didn't show on the surface and hadn't been present in his tone when he talked to Bridie. Nonetheless, underneath his aloof exterior, he nursed a terrible fury.

She used the tinted spectacles as a shield to study him. He wore a slate gray suit edged with black leather piping and a plain black waistcoat. The garments had been well made but were now out of fashion and the fit almost indecently snug. He wore no jewelry, not even a watch chain. His linen shirt was modestly ruffled, brilliant white against his bronzed complexion. Dark brown eyes reflected a guarded expression, one of keen, quick assessment. At first, she'd thought his hair was as black as her own, but the color of his was more like coffee.

His smile was his most disarming feature. This she learned when he turned slightly in her direction. Under the shadow of a luxuriant mustache, he gave her a grin full of confidence and conceit, slow and mocking, as he exposed most of his strong, white teeth in her direction. She hadn't thought she could press any harder against the back of the chair but she did.

A snarl. The man is snarling a challenge.

"Sit down, Jake," his brother said in lieu of a pleasant greeting.

Mr. Williams hesitated, glancing her way, as if seeking her permission. When she didn't respond, he offered her a slight nod and sat. The chair protested his sturdy bulk.

Again came that niggling, internal note of caution. Something wasn't quite right. She'd expected someone uncouth, and Williams was not. He'd just proved it. If a lady didn't wish to be acknowledged, it was a gentleman's duty to respect her wish. He'd done so in a manner suave and subtle—a startling and unexpected display of parlor manners in a man from the unprincipled West.

She had only moments to discover if Williams could be her salvation or ruination. Harold's description of his brother was far off the mark. Prejudice created this gross error in assessment. What if faulty judgment enhanced his half-brother's skills?

Harold stood and tugged down his waistcoat hem. "Now, Jake, we know why you are here."

Sarcastic and defensive, Williams murmured, "Do we, Harold?"

"We discussed the particulars yesterday. I spoke with Schwartzstein this morning. He has agreed to terms. He won't press charges and has promised not to retaliate. We can move forward if certain conditions are met by no later than four of the afternoon, tomorrow."

When Williams said nothing and continued to stare at his sibling, Harold cleared his throat and primly readjusted his spectacles. He remained standing to maintain the impression of authority. Unfortunately, this tactic fooled no one.

"As you well know, Jake, we are here to finalize the particulars of the contract between Mrs. Corday and yourself. Upon signing this document," he slid the papers forward, "arrangements will be made to have your cattle paid for and delivered to the railroad of your choice. The gambling debt with Schwartzstein we have previously discussed. Pen and ink are there. It's all very simple. All that's required is your signature."

Williams negligently glanced through the document, ready to set it aside, then something within caught his attention. She knew exactly what that was. Squashing a surge of humiliation, she watched him thoughtlessly withdraw a pair of gold-rimmed spectacles from his coat's inner breast pocket. She found it unnerving that he could look even more attractive with the glasses on his once-broken nose.

Before he commenced reading, he glared over the wire rims to ask, "Are you sure this is the smallest print you could find?"

Harold shrugged and said down his nose, "Newsprint type from Mrs. Corday's publishing firm."

Williams arched a dark eyebrow and returned to the agreement. The silence in the room intensified. His lips tightened as he read. He returned the spectacles to his pocket.

The document skidded across the gleaming desktop when he tossed it back with contempt. "You sure you got the numbers right, Harold? Twenty thousand upon the satisfactory completion of my term of employment, which will be determined by my employer? That's a lot of money for a hired gun."

"That's because the position entrails considerably more than the mere protection of my employer. There's Mrs. Corday's standing in the community to consider."

"You aren't answering the question, Harold. And what's that bit of muck about complying and adapting to any and all extenuating conditions as needed?"

Harold fidgeted and touched the document. "As an added precaution and further assurance of my client's safety, it has been decided that she must be married."

"Yeah? So?"

"To you,"

The slow burn she suspected smoldered just under the surface flared to life when Williams came up out of his chair. He planted his fists on the desk and leaned over to stick his face close to his brother's.

In a grating, growling tone, Williams said, "I've been coerced, insulted, and humiliated, much to your never ending delight, but *this* is stepping over the line."

Harold relaxed his lips from its prim, little moue. "Not at all. And I should think you'd leap at the chance of marriage to a lady of Mrs. Corday's stature and background."

She winced when Williams snapped, "The wife of the sleaziest criminal in town and a divorcee?"

"Jake, if it's not too far beyond your limited understanding, you should've noted that despite those drawbacks, none of which were within her control, she has managed to become a most respected member of Chicago society."

"If a lady were not present, Harold, I'd tell you exactly what I think of your precious Chicago society and where you can insert your servile notions."

While the brothers squabbled, her impatience
214

swelled. Usually calm and clever while negotiating, Harold had lost control of the interview. And what had happened to the exaggerated western accent or the sweetly lascivious drawl Williams had used on Bridie?

Sweat rolled off Harold's temple. His nasal voice gathered pitch and venom as he stated, "Before you start whining about the loss of your precious freedom, for we know that your inability to commit to anything of import is what this protest is all about, you may be assured that the marriage will be temporary."

Williams paused, creating an uncomfortable silence. He straightened up from the desk and rolled his shoulders. "So, you're saying the marriage will be fake."

"No, it will be quite legal, but you'll be required to adhere to certain conditions and restrictions."

Williams studied his brother until an idea changed his expression from indignation to a gloating delight more unsettling that his outrage. He returned to his chair and lazily sat. "Conditions? And what restrictions, Harold? I'll need some clarification. You'll have to be precise. My limited intellect requires an explicit explanation.